AT THE SIGN OF THE
GOLDEN PINEAPPLE

Henrietta Bascombe's friends gasped when she talked about going into trade. For Henrietta was hell-bent on opening a sweet shop to rival the famous Gunther's.

The shop prospered and earned the custom of the entire haute ton that is until the Earl of Carrisdowne took exception to his brother ogling the girls behind Bascombe's counter, and decided it must be put out of business quickly.

But somehow the earl looked forward to tangling with the fiery Miss Bascombe much more than he was willing to admit....

AT THE SIGN OF THE
GOLDEN PINEAPPLE

At The Sign
Of The
Golden Pineapple

by
Marion Chesney

MAGNA PRINT BOOKS
Long Preston, North Yorkshire,
England.

British Library Cataloguing in Publication Data.

Chesney, Marion
   At the sign of the golden pineapple.
   I. Title
   823.914 (F)

   ISBN 0-7505-0151-0
   ISBN 0-7505-0255-X pbk

First Published in Great Britain by Severn House Publishers Ltd.,
1990.

Copyright © 1987 by Marion Chesney

Published in Large Print 1991 by arrangement with Severn House
Publishers Ltd., London.

Printed and bound in Great Britain by
T.J. Press (Padstow) Ltd., Cornwall, PL28 8RW.

All the characters in this book are fictitious, and any resemblance to persons living or dead is purely coincidental.

For Maria Browne
With love

CHAPTER ONE

Miss Henrietta Bascombe and Miss Ismene Hissop stood with candle-lighters at the ready, waiting for the sounds of the arrival of their first guest.

Unthinkable that they should light the candles beforehand. Henrietta and Miss Hissop were both well-versed in every penny-pinching way of impoverished gentility.

Although it was winter, the fire had not yet been lighted. Warmth also, had to wait for the guests.

Henrietta had lately inherited a 'fortune'—five thousand pounds *was* a fortune after years of trying to make ends meet—but she did not want to waste a penny of it.

Her father had been a country doctor who had earned so little that he had often acted as vet to supplement his small income. When he had died, he had left Henrietta his small house and pocket-size garden and very little money. With the sensible view that two impoverished ladies can live together more cheaply than in separate households, Henrietta had offered a home to her old friend and former school-teacher, Miss Hissop.

Together they had worked at trying to exist on as little as possible while keeping up appearances. They wore cotton dresses instead of silk, claiming they preferred washable materials; they bought yesterday's bread from the bakers 'to feed the birds,' and gave genteel card-parties, where, with grim determination and flushed faces, they played for shillings and sixpences as if they were the most dedicated gamblers of St James's, playing for thousands.

The 'fortune' had come as a great surprise. The money had been left to Henrietta by the local landowner, Sir Benjamin Prestcott, in his will. He had turned religious before his death and, conscience-stricken that he had never paid Henrietta's father for any of that poor man's excellent services, he had decided to make amends by leaving Henrietta the money with a view to providing her with a dowry.

But Henrietta had other plans for the money. So the evening's entertainment was not just a tea party. It was to be more like a council of war.

For Henrietta meant to go into trade.

In vain had Miss Hissop protested. Henrietta was determined to open a confectioner's in London's West End, and nothing Miss Hissop could say would move her from that resolve.

Henrietta would need shop assistants, and the best London confectioners always had the prettiest of girls. To that end, she had invited two ladies from the neighbourhood to tea, knowing they were unhappy with their present life, and confident they would enjoy the chance to share this new adventure with her.

In them lay Miss Hissop's last hope. Both ladies were of the gentry, and she was sure their horror at Henrietta's suggestion would change that determined lady's mind.

It was not as if dear Henrietta could not get a husband easily, thought Miss Hissop. Henrietta had dark-brown glossy hair that curled naturally, a trim figure, and wide brown eyes. But Henrietta would point out that the only eligible men in the village of Partlett were antidotes. Miss Hissop could see nothing wrong with the eligibles the village had to offer.

Men were men, and it really didn't matter what they looked like. Miss Hissop often found it hard to tell them apart.

A reddish sun sparkled over the frost on the garden outside. Miss Hissop shivered, wishing the guests would arrive so that they could light the fire.

And then they were there, coming up the garden path, Mrs Charlotte Webster and Miss

Josephine Archer.

The small, dark parlour was bathed in a soft light as Miss Hissop and Henrietta lighted the candles. Then the fire gave a cheerful crackle, and the first flames shot up to disperse the bone-chilling cold of the room.

Miss Hissop removed her large woollen shawl and hurried to answer the door.

'Welcome,' she said to the two ladies on the step. 'Come in. Such a bore having to answer the door oneself, but our Martha has gone to visit her mother.'

Miss Hissop's servant Martha was a pure fiction. Neither she nor Henrietta had ever had a servant. This was a fact well-known in the little village, but Miss Hissop had persuaded herself that everyone actually believed in the perpetually absent Martha.

Henrietta studied them with a calculating eye. Yes, they were both as pretty as she had remembered them to be, although she had not seen either since the death of her father.

Josephine was the daughter of the local squire, a chestnut-haired beauty dressed in scarlet merino. It was hard to tell from her fashionable clothes and calm, beautiful face that she led the life of a dog with her widower father, who cursed her and beat her every time he was in his cups, which was often.

14

Charlotte was too thin for true beauty, and had high cheekbones, a definite setback in an age where women deliberately rounded their cheeks by stuffing them with wax pads. But she had beautiful black hair, and her eyes were sapphire. She had a natural grace and elegance.

She had married an undistinguished army captain and been thrown out by her family for doing so. The captain had died, leaving her with only an army widow's pension.

Henrietta did not know them as friends, only as former patients of her father. Josephine had been treated for cracked ribs after one of her father's more severe beatings and Charlotte for fainting fits, which turned out to have been brought on by semi-starvation.

Usually Henrietta served tiny sandwiches—yesterday's bread being carefully damped to make it appear fresh—and minuscule tea cakes.

As soon as the ladies were seated, she surprised them by serving soup laced with wine, followed by peasant-size sandwiches filled with beef.

Watching delicate colour beginning to come into Charlotte's thin cheeks, Henrietta talked of this and that and held her fire until she was sure they were all thoroughly warmed.

Without opening her mouth, Miss Hissop was sending out distress signals. Her weak eyes

15

pleaded with Henrietta to abandon the vulgar idea of trade.

Miss Hissop was much addicted to wearing cravats and jockey caps and gave all the appearance of a strong-minded woman. She was in her forties and had a harsh-featured face, weak eyes, and a thin mouth that turned down at the corners.

Only Henrietta knew that behind this formidable exterior lurked the soul of a rabbit. All Miss Hissop wanted out of life was to pay for her own funeral and not to be buried in a pauper's grave. In the way that young girls had a 'bottom drawer' or wedding chest for their trousseau, Miss Hissop had a funeral closet in which she kept the little money she had saved in a tin box, a hand-embroidered shroud, black armbands for the mourners, and a long list of instructions as to the funeral arrangements.

Henrietta waited until tea had been poured and then rapped her spoon against the side of her cup for silence. Charlotte and Josephine, who had been discussing knitting patterns, broke off and looked at her in surprise.

'I have invited you here for a reason,' said Henrietta.

'I am sure, my dear, Mrs Webster and Miss Archer accepted your invitation to *tea*, you know, because ladies take *tea* and do not

16

do...other things,' said Miss Hissop inco-
herently.

Henrietta ignored her. 'I have been left five
thousand pounds in Sir Benjamin Prestcott's
will. He was my father's patient, you know.'

The ladies murmured their congratulations.

'I do not mean to use the money as a dowry,'
said Henrietta.

'More tea?' bleated Miss Hissop. 'You will
feel so much more rational after tea, Henrietta.'

'I mean,' said Henrietta firmly, 'to go into
trade.'

'But there is no need for that,' said Charlotte,
wide-eyed.

'There are no men in this village I would
even *look* at,' said Henrietta.

'But with a dowry like that,' protested
Josephine, 'you could go to some spa and attend balls and parties. There are plenty of eligible gentlemen at the spas. Tunbridge Wells,
for example, is not so expensive as Bath.'

'There you are!' exclaimed Miss Hissop,
beaming all around. '*Just* what I said.'

'I do not think I want to *have* to marry,' said
Henrietta. 'I do not think I want to be married *at all.*'

'In that case,' said Charlotte, 'five thousand
pounds properly invested would keep you in
relative comfort.'

'But that is not the case,' said Henrietta. 'I want to be rich. Very rich. Now, merchants take sums of money and turn them into *more* money. We all have a talent. Everyone has some talent, but women are never allowed to exploit it. I, for example, am a first-class confectioner and baker.'

There was a murmur of assent. Henrietta could conjure delicacies out of next-to-nothing. Charlotte still remembered Henrietta arriving with her father when he had attended her, bearing a small bottle of cordial and two slices of delicious home-baked cake.

'Therefore,' Henrietta went on, 'I wish to lease premises in the West End of London and start my own confectioner's shop. I mean to rival Gunter's.'

Gunter's was the Almack's of the confectioners' trade. Situated in Berkeley Square, it attracted all the members of the ton, and Gunter's ices were legendary.

'No, I do not mean to serve ices,' said Henrietta although no one had spoken. 'Not at first. I could not afford shipments of ice from Greenland like Gunter.'

'I see you have asked us here for advice,' said Josephine, with a sympathetic look at Miss Hissop.

'It is just *not done*. What if your venture did

not succeed? What gentleman would entertain the idea of marriage to you after you had been in trade?'

'Perhaps a merchant,' said Henrietta sharply. 'I am tired of gentility. Look at my poor father's life. *Never* would he press for payment, because a gentleman did not do that sort of thing. Although he was from a landed family, he was nevertheless only a country doctor, whereas Mama was the *daughter* of the Honourable Edward Devere, and people told her and *told her* she had married beneath her, until she made father's life a misery, and I *swear* she died of discontent!'

'Henrietta!' exclaimed Miss Hissop. 'Your poor, dear mama!'

Henrietta turned red. 'I am sorry, but I only speak the truth. We are all kept in chains by the fact that we are genteel women. Let me speak plain. You, Charlotte, could do with three good meals a day. You were considered to have married beneath you, and so your family has cast you off. Josephine—well, the least said about Squire Archer the better. He would not treat a son thus...or a horse. No, I am determined to make my own way in life. If I am going to be a social outcast, I shall be a *rich* social outcast.'

'But,' said Charlotte timidly, 'it appears you

did not, after all, ask us here for advice. So why...?'

'I am about to come to that. Now, everyone knows a good confectioner's has the prettiest of girls. You and Miss Archer are both beautiful, and so...'

'You are never suggesting that Mrs Webster and myself should serve behind a *counter?*' said Josephine, two spots of colour burning on her cheeks.

'Yes,' said Henrietta baldly. 'I am offering you both jobs. I shall put up the money, and the profits will be divided among the four of us.'

'The four!' squeaked Miss Hissop. 'Dear Henrietta, it never crossed my mind that you would expect me to *work!*'

'Working in a successful business in London is surely better than living in this backwater,' said Henrietta roundly.

Charlotte's long, white, almost transparent fingers fluttered helplessly. 'I am sorry, Miss Bascombe,' she said in a stifled voice. 'It was good of you to ask me, but I must refuse.'

'And I,' said Josephine firmly, rising and drawing on her gloves. 'I am sure that when you think calmly about the matter, you will find it would not serve. Only very common people go into business.'

'I am before my time,' said Henrietta sadly. 'I am sorry you will not be joining me in my venture, but I shall go ahead alone if need be.'

The two now highly embarrassed ladies found their shawls. With many flurried and hurried good-byes, they made their way out into the freezing cold of the late afternoon.

'Oooof!' said Henrietta, retreating to the parlour and sinking down into a battered horsehair armchair in front of the fire. 'They *were* shocked.'

'And quite rightly, too,' said Miss Hissop. 'Let us go to bed early tonight, Henrietta. I am persuaded you need more rest.'

'We always go to bed early,' said Henrietta gloomily. 'We've never, until the windfall, been able to burn candles after the sun goes down. But, in any case, I shall need a good night's rest. It's a ten mile walk in the morning to meet the stage at Oaktree crossroads.

'Where are you going?'

Henrietta yawned. 'I am going to London to lease premises for a shop.'

'Oh, no,' moaned Miss Hissop. 'Only bad can come of this idea. I am glad, yes, *glad*, that neither Mrs Webster nor Miss Archer encouraged you in your folly.'

'They have not had time to think about it,'

pointed out Henrietta. 'They may yet come about.'

'Not them,' said Miss Hissop with conviction. 'Certainly not them!'

Later that evening, Josephine Archer lay in her bed, a handkerchief soaked in cologne held against one bruised cheek. Squire Archer had been drunk when she returned from Henrietta's. She had not been expecting him to be home and had therefore been taken aback by his sudden drunken appearance in the drawing room. She had let her contempt and disgust for him, usually so carefully concealed, show in her eyes. And the furious squire had struck her in the face with his fist.

Josephine eventually dried her eyes and thought about her strange conversation with Henrietta. She began to wonder if she herself would ever marry. Unlike Henrietta, Josephine had found several gentlemen in the village and local county quite pleasing.

But her father's mad drunken rages had driven away any suitable callers.

Henrietta might be lowering herself to go into trade but she would be in *London*, not hidden away in some English village, dreading the sound of her own father's voice.

Father would chase her to London in any

case, thought Josephine dismally. But just suppose Henrietta had not told anyone else other than Miss Hissop or herself or Charlotte what she planned to do. Then it would be possible to leave a note for the squire saying she had run off to Scotland with some man. Just suppose...

Josephine sat bolt upright in bed. Henrietta's offer, which had seemed so outrageous earlier in the day, now seemed like a golden chance of freedom. If only Henrietta had not told anyone else.

Charlotte Webster awoke during the night and lay shivering under her thin blankets. Food. Mountains of food. That's what she had been dreaming of. A confectioner's. She could see it now, the golden pineapple over the door, the piles of oranges and pineapples and dainty cakes. The smells of hot chocolate and coffee. Her stomach growled ferociously.

That is what maintaining the status of the lady of the parish does for me, thought Charlotte bitterly. All I have to show for my gentle birth is a rumbling stomach and a freezing bedroom and winter days stretching out to an infinity of more rumbling stomachs and more freezing nights.

She had once been a plump headstrong girl,

but hunger and more hunger had broken her spirit.

Somewhere inside her, that old rebellious Charlotte was beginning to argue, was beginning to say in a louder and louder voice, 'Go to London. Go to London. Go to London, you widgeon. No one will miss you. You can *eat*. Even if the business is a failure, you will be able to eat while it lasts. Go to London!'

Henrietta, setting out the next day for the long walk to meet the stage, had two notes handed to her, one by the squire's footman, the other by a village boy.

The first was from Josephine. In it she said she would go with Henrietta and work for her provided that no one in the village, especially not her father, should find out her whereabouts. The second was from Charlotte Webster. The paper was blotted with tears, and the note said pathetically, 'Thank you. I must accept your offer. I am so very hungry.'

Henrietta retreated indoors to tell the startled Miss Hissop the good news and warn her to tell no one at all about the venture. Miss Hissop dumbly shook her head. She had never mentioned a word to anyone, hoping against hope that Henrietta would change her mind before she disgraced herself.

Henrietta set out again. The day was glittering with frost, but the sky was blue, and the sparkling, shining road led straight as an arrow out of the village of Partlett.

'Success is coming,' said Henrietta to herself. 'I can *feel* it.'

CHAPTER TWO

'What is so vastly interesting in the existence of a new confectioner's?' asked the Earl of Carrisdowne.

His friend, Mr Guy Clifford, neatly guided his curricle between a Covent Garden cart and a hackney carriage before replying. 'Nothing. If it were an ordinary confectioner's, that is. What makes Bascombe's so interesting is that Miss Bascombe is a brown-haired beauty.'

'Nothing unusual in that,' remarked the earl. 'Confectioners are famous for their beautiful girls.'

'But this one *is* Bascombe's, if you take my meaning. She started the business a month ago. And she's gently bred, and so are her two female assistants.'

'It is not out of the way for shopkeepers to

claim gentility,' said the earl. 'You know that, Guy.'

'But, damme, you've only got to look at 'em, *speak* to 'em. They've even got a dragon of a lady to keep an eye on 'em.'

'Are you trying to tell me that these tonnish ladies have taken to *trade?*' demanded the earl.

'Well, I suppose that's it,' said Mr Clifford awkwardly. 'Ain't that just what I've been saying?'

The earl cast a cold blue eye on his friend. 'I thought you were looking for a wife, not a mistress,' he remarked.

Mr Clifford flushed. 'Surely running a respectable establishment like a confectioner's don't put a female beyond the pale?'

'Yes, it does, my friend,' said the earl gently. 'And well you know it.'

Mr Clifford set his lips in a mutinous line. Rupert, Earl of Carrisdowne, was his friend, not his guardian. But sometimes the earl went on like a guardian or a parent.

He forgot how many times the earl had pulled him out of dangerous scrapes when he was younger. The earl, like Mr Clifford, had recently returned from the wars in the peninsula, the earl because of the death of his father, which meant he inherited the earldom, and Mr Clifford because of a shrapnel wound. They had

26

not seen much of each other during the past five years, having been in different regiments. Mr Clifford was now twenty-nine. He had a comfortable income from a small Kentish estate and planned to find a wife and settle down.

The earl had readily agreed to enjoy the delights of London in Mr Clifford's company. He was tired of war and wanted a period of relaxation before sinking himself into the cares of his estates.

He was a tall, broad-shouldered man burned brown by the Spanish sun. He had a thin, high-bridged nose and a firm mouth. His clothes were faultless, and Guy reflected enviously that the earl managed to achieve in half an hour what it took him, Guy, a good half day to accomplish.

The earl's coats lay across his shoulders without a single wrinkle, cravats fell into intricate, sculptured perfection under his fingers, and his breeches hugged his thighs like a second skin. His boots never had a mark on their glossy surface, even in the muddiest of weather.

Guy was a contrast to his tall, black-haired autocratic-looking friend. He had a fair, pleasant face and steady grey eyes. He was stocky and of only medium height.

Despite his longing for sartorial elegance, his clothes seemed to have a mind of their own.

27

After a bare hour of leaving the hands of his valet, his waistcoat would start to ride up, and his shirt would bunch out over his breeches. The strings of his breeches would untie themselves at his knees, and the starch would mysteriously disappear from his cravat.

And yet Guy, who often resented the earl's high-handed manner and puritanical views, found that the comradeship of more easygoing friends always seemed to lead to marked cards and fast women. Despite his rather rakish past, he was a romantic at heart and was determined to fall in love when the Season started, get married, and live happily ever after.

No one could accuse the earl of being romantic. No beauty had been able to light a spark in his black, cynical eyes. At the age of thirty-three, he was still unmarried. Guy pitied the woman the earl would eventually take as a wife. He was convinced the earl would lead her a dog's life.

The earl, meanwhile, was making a mental note to have a look at this Bascombe's. It would be just like Guy to fall in love with a shop girl.

But when he made a few discreet enquiries that evening, it was to find that no one seemed to have actually gone *into* Bascombe's—only doubtfully admiring the ladies from afar.

Gunter's was the fashionable place, and no

one could see any reason to go anywhere else.

'Doom and disaster,' sighed Miss Henrietta Bascombe to herself as she looked out at the bleak February day. Only two months until the Season started and, unless a miracle happened, they would need to lock up the shop and go home.

Over the doorway of Bascombe's in Half Moon Street swung a golden pineapple, the sign that hung outside all good confectioners.

Inside were the most delicious cakes and confections imaginable. But the little tables stood empty, and the fashionable throng drifted past with only brief curious looks.

Henrietta, Charlotte and Josephine were all dressed alike in striped cotton gowns and muslin aprons. Little lace caps with jaunty streamers ornamented their heads. Charlotte had put on some much-needed weight, for often they ate some of their stock at the end of the day before delivering the rest to the foundling hospital.

Henrietta did not want to leave London, particularly when things were looking so hopeful for Josephine. One of their very, very few customers, a Mr Guy Clifford, had seemed enchanted with Josephine, and Henrietta had liked his easy, open manner.

As she stood by the window of the shop, a pale-faced young man hesitated outside. While Henrietta sent up a silent prayer, he took a few steps away, then turned back, and opened the door.

Henrietta went forward to serve him. 'Just some hot chocolate,' he murmured, sitting down at a little table and burying his face in his hands.

Henrietta rushed to prepare a cup of chocolate and then set the steaming liquid down in front of him.

He winced as if she had presented him with a cup of poison, turned a greenish colour, muttered, 'I can't. The brandy, you know. Oh, my cursed head,' and stumbled to his feet and lurched out of the shop.

'What on earth was the matter with *him?*' asked Josephine, round-eyed.

'He, like most gentlemen in Mayfair, is suffering from having drunk too long and too deeply the night before,' said Henrietta crossly. 'Perhaps I should have opened an apothecary's...' Her voice trailed away as an idea struck her. 'That's it,' she breathed. 'That's *it!*'

'I am glad you have realized that that is it,' said Miss Hissop, who had emerged from the back shop in time to hear Henrietta's words.

'Now that you have come to your senses, we can all pack up and go home.'

'No, no. I mean I have hit on a plan to get the fashionables to patronize us,' said Henrietta, her eyes glowing. 'I still have Papa's book, where he has his recipes for various cordials, highly efficacious for the treatment of a disordered stomach and spleen. If I put them in the window with an advertisement, *that* will fetch them!'

'Nothing will fetch them,' said Miss Hissop. 'We are unfashionables, as I knew we should be. Dear Henrietta, let us return to our little home. I do not wish to die in London. London undertakers are *so* expensive. And in London, it costs *one shilling an hour* to hire a mute.'

Miss Hissop's morbid preoccupation with her own funeral often irritated Henrietta who, like all young people, thought of herself as immortal. But this new idea was burning in her brain, and she was too anxious to begin to make up the medicines and cordials to become annoyed with her spinster friend.

She worked far into the night while the other ladies went to bed in a sort of dormitory above the shop.

At last she was finished. She felt exhausted because she had had to walk to visit the herbal shops and apothecaries over in the city the previous afternoon. There was still one thing to be done, the all-important one—how to word the advertisement that was to stand in front of the bottles in the window.

It was no use hinting at the problems these prescriptions were supposed to cure. Gentlemen were too fuzzy in their heads in the morning to deal with subtleties. Taking a deep breath, she printed carefully,

BASCOMBE'S ELIXIRS.
FOR DISORDERS OF THE SPLEEN
CAUSED
BY OVERINDULGENCE.

Was that too rude? Too blunt? Henrietta nervously chewed the end of her quill and then had to pick bits of feather out of her mouth.

'I shall leave it,' she decided. 'Should it prove too blunt and no one takes the bait, I shall rephrase it.'

After some two hours' sleep, she awoke and roused the others. The day's baking had to commence, just as if they were expecting a flood of customers. There was always hope.

The elderly Duke of Gillingham picked his way homeward along Half Moon Street the following morning at eleven o'clock. He had been drinking and gambling at Watier's club at the corner of Bolton Street and Piccadilly. A large breakfast, which usually put him to rights, had failed to work its magic.

His head felt hot and fevered and his stomach queasy. He felt he wanted to go home, summon his lawyers, and dictate his last will and testament. His tongue felt like a Turkish carpet that had had cigar ash spilled on it.

He was about to pass what he privately termed 'that jolly little confectioner's with the pretty gels.' He was often tempted to go in. But *no one* went there. It was as simple as that.

He stopped a few paces on and looked thoughtfully at the ground. Then he walked back again and raised his quizzing glass. He leaned forward, was overtaken by a sudden fit of dizziness, and banged his head against the glass. Cursing horribly, he straightened up and slowly and painfully scrutinized the advertisement.

Like a sleepwalker, he mounted the shallow steps, opened the door, and went in. He almost fled before the nauseating smells of sugar and cinnamon and chocolate.

'May I help you, sir?'

There was a dainty brunette in a striped gown and apron and a delicious frivolity of a cap curtsying before him.

'Bascombe's Elixir...fast,' grated the duke

33

in a rusty voice.

'Yes, sir,' said Henrietta.

'Yes, *your grace*,' whispered Miss Hissop, who had made it her business to discover who was who in the West End of London.

Henrietta placed the duke at a seat by the window. She poured a small bottle of the cordial into a glass and handed it to him.

He looked at her doubtfully with his red-rimmed eyes. Then he jerked the contents down his throat and placed both hands on the table and hung on.

A warm glow spread throughout his stomach. A feeling of well-being began to permeate his whole system. He shook his head as if to clear it and looked around slowly, a little colour beginning to tinge his yellowish face.

What a charming place it was, he thought with a sort of wonder. How good everything smelled! Charlotte and Josephine came in from the back shop bearing trays of cakes. What beauties, breathed the duke.

Now Henrietta had another powerful advertisement to add to the one already in the window. The Duke of Gillingham was seated at the window of the confectioner's in full view of anyone passing. He asked for chocolate and flirted amiably with Charlotte and Josephine.

One by one more gentlemen came in to take

the cure and stayed to chat with Henrietta, Charlotte, and Josephine.

By the time the ladies of Mayfair set out on their calls, every fashionable man in London seemed to be crammed into Bascombe's.

The ladies could not find places, and so they were determined to get to Bascombe's the next day *before* the gentlemen arrived. A confectioner's was the only place where two ladies could meet for tea and cakes unescorted. And with all these gentlemen, it now looked a better prospect for attracting a suitable beau than Almack's.

Guy Clifford, arriving at his usual time of three in the afternoon, found he had to stand outside on the pavement and wait for a free seat.

Gloomily he watched through the window as various gentlemen ogled and stared at Josephine, and ground his teeth. She should not be subjected to such vulgar company. How he longed to take her away from it all.

He flushed guiltily when he heard himself being hailed and turned and saw the willowy figure of the Earl of Carrisdowne's younger brother, Lord Charles Worsley.

'What are you hanging around here for?' asked Lord Charles curiously.

'Waiting for a place,' mumbled Mr Clifford,

wondering what the earl would say if Charles told him where he had found him. 'Oh, look,' said Mr Clifford suddenly, 'those two Bond Street fribbles are just leaving. Come along.' He seized Lord Charles's arm and all but dragged him inside.

'What's all the fuss? Why all the stampede?' asked Lord Charles. He was as black-haired and high-nosed as his brother, but where the earl's expression was autocratic and harsh, Lord Charles's was innocent and guileless.

'I don't know,' said Mr Clifford, who had been too busy watching for glimpses of Josephine to read the advertisement. 'It's worse than a rout.'

Charlotte curtsied before them. 'What is your pleasure, gentlemen?' she asked.

'I don't know,' said Lord Charles. 'I was *dragged* in here, so to speak. I know, I'll have one of your wet confects.'

Confectioners sold wet or dry confects. The wet ones were various fruits immersed in liquid syrup; the dry, apart from cakes and biscuits, were little figures or houses or ships made out of marzipan or fruit, beaten into a paste with sugar.

Charlotte described the various varieties of wet confects, and Lord Charles settled for apricot. Mr Clifford asked for turtle soup.

Charlotte blushed prettily. All good confectioners sold turtle soup, but since they had had no customers for it, it was an expensive business to keep making pots of turtle soup and then being forced to give it away, and so they no longer had any in stock.

'Not today, sir,' she said.

'He'll have the same as me,' said Lord Charles cheerfully. And as Charlotte walked away, he said to Mr Clifford, 'I'll eat yours if you don't want it. Couldn't stand to see her blush. Pretty girl. *Very* pretty girl. Do you see that beautiful shine on her black hair?'

'I say,' said Mr Clifford, hitching his chair closer to the table, 'you know how authoritative Rupert can be at times.'

'My brother can be a deemed bully, if that's what you mean,' said Lord Charles with feeling.

'Yes, well, I told him about Bascombe's and how odd it was they were all *ladies*. He disapproved. Said they couldn't be ladies if they were working in a shop. Told him that little Miss Bascombe over there who can't be more than twenty opened up the business herself. He gave me a cold look—I was driving at the time, and I swear I felt the chill from it going right down one side—and more or less told me I was making a cake of myself. *You* know.'

'So you don't want me to tell him you've been seen here,' grinned Lord Charles. 'Tell you what, we *both* shan't tell him we've been here, and we can enjoy the company of these pretty ladies undisturbed. Now, which one is it? Miss Bascombe, the one with the chestnut hair or the beautiful princess in the tower who is serving us?'

'No one in particular,' said Mr Clifford airily. 'Ain't much interested in ladies these days, to tell the truth.'

He turned and found Josephine at his elbow and flushed brick-red.

'Oho!' grinned Lord Charles maliciously. 'The truth, is it?'

Instead of waiting wearily until ten in the evening in the hope of a customer, Henrietta was able to put up the heavy shutters at six. She went back into the shop and looked with dazed delight at the empty shelves. Then she groaned. It was going to be another long night of baking, and brewing elixir.

Charlotte and Josephine were sitting in chairs in the shop, looking weary but triumphant. Miss Hissop was counting out the day's takings and dreaming of a magnificent funeral with plumed horses and paid mourners.

'We should have helped you with the

shutters,' yawned Josephine. 'In fact, the sooner we hire a man, the better. It is heavy work stoking the fires for the ovens and cleaning up.'

'I am very strong,' said Henrietta, 'though I do feel a little weak at the moment. I must sit down and get out the order book. We are going to need large quantities of *everything*. Yes, you are right. We *do* need a boy to fetch and carry for us. Perhaps on Sunday I shall go to the nearest workhouse and see if I can find someone.'

'The workhouse!' shuddered Miss Hissop, her hands full of sovereigns and silver. 'Much safer to get a young man from one of the agencies.'

'No,' said Henrietta. 'It is a chance to allow some poor boy from the workhouse a comfortable living. We are a success, ladies! Bascombe's has become fashionable.

'Nothing can stop our success now!'

A week later, the Earl of Carrisdowne stood outside Bascombe's and looked in. His younger brother and his best friend were cozily ensconced in a corner, gazing at two of the young shopgirls in a decidedly spoony manner.

He walked on, thoroughly irritated. His brother and Mr Clifford were notoriously gullible when it came to the fair sex. Had not Guy nearly proposed marriage once to a member of the fashionable impure whom Guy had persuaded himself was really an innocent virgin?

And had not young Charles run off with an opera dancer? And would have married the trollop had he, the earl, not been home on leave to put a stop to the romance?

Nonetheless, he had almost decided to leave the matter of Bascombe's until things became more obviously serious but changed his mind because of the involvement with that wretched place of another member of the family.

His young sister, Lady Sarah Worsley, had been steadily growing as fat as a pig. She was just seventeen and had an enormous appetite for cakes. When the earl had pointed out that she was ruining her face and figure with sweetmeats, she had gone on a strict diet for a while and had emerged as a pretty girl. Now she was fat and spotty again, and he soon learned the problem was Bascombe's. Lady Sarah stated she had never tasted such delicious cakes before. The earl forbade her to visit Bascombe's, an order that Lady Sarah accepted with uncharacteristic meekness. Then it transpired that she had simply been sending round a footman each day with a long list of all the cakes she craved.

The Earl of Carrisdowne turned over the problem of Bascombe's in his mind. What a pity the wretched place had become fashionable.

Then his face cleared.

Although he had never *tried* to be a leader of fashion, he was, nevertheless, because of the elegance of his clothes and the haughtiness of his manner, already looked up to as an arbiter of fashion.

He would make Bascombe's unfashionable.

A little word dropped here. A little word there.

It was all very simple.

CHAPTER THREE

The Earl of Carrisdowne was to be seen gracing many balls and parties during the following week.

He always managed to turn the conversation to Bascombe's. 'You like the place? How odd. I thought only peasants and mushrooms went there,' he said.

Until the full force of his social disapproval hit Bascombe's, Henrietta, flushed and happy, did a roaring trade.

She had employed a boy from the workhouse. He was an ill-favoured lad of fourteen called Esau. Esau had a bad squint that gave him a cunning look, belying the gentle soul within. To have been transported from a miserable life to a West End confectioner's, to be able to eat cake for the first time in his life, persuaded the deeply religious Esau that all his prayers had been answered.

Even Miss Hissop, who had not at first approved of the boy, had her heart melted by the vast amount of work he did. Esau slaved early and late. No more did Henrietta have to nurse an aching back after stoking the bakery fires or taking down and putting up the heavy shutters. Esau was thin and round-shouldered. But he was very wiry and strong and could run like the wind.

He was to be dressed in red-plush livery as soon as his new suit of clothes arrived from the tailor, and he was to have his hair powdered.

The Duchess of Gillingham had ordered a centrepiece from Bascombe's for a dinner party. It was Henrietta's first order, and she planned to make it the talk of London.

The first signs of disaster came one day the following week. By noontime, although many gentlemen had hurried in to buy Bascombe's elixir, none had stayed to drink it. Instead, they took the bottles with them, slinking in and out of the shop with a furtive air.

Henrietta did not know that Mr Clifford and Lord Charles had gone into the country to attend a prize fight, and so she thought they had deserted her as well.

Then the final blow fell. The Duchess of Gillingham sent a servant, cancelling the order for the centrepiece.

Gloomily Henrietta told Esau to put up the shutters at six in the evening. Then she called a council of war.

'What has happened?' she demanded. 'Why are we become unfashionable again?'

'London society is fickle,' wailed Miss Hissop. 'Do let us leave this dreadful place before we lose any more money, Henrietta.'

'No,' said Henrietta, her soft mouth setting in a stubborn line. 'Mr Clifford seemed much taken with you, Josephine, and Lord Charles with Charlotte. Why have they suddenly sheered off?'

'I am suddenly so very tired,' said Charlotte listlessly. 'I was kept going by the excitement of success. I cannot *bear* to think of making and baking cakes again for people who do not come. Now, even the duchess has cancelled her order. Could you have done it anyway, Henrietta? It is very difficult to make one of those elaborate centrepieces.'

'Yes, I could have done it; better than Gunter's, too,' said Henrietta. 'Sir Benjamin Prestcott's chef used to let me watch how he created miracles out of spun sugar. I would spend my time with him in the kitchen while Papa was attending Sir Benjamin. He was a Frenchman who had escaped the Terror. He was an artist.'

'Something has gone badly wrong,' said Josephine, wrinkling her smooth brow. 'Do you think someone had a disordered stomach after eating here and talked of it?'

'No,' said Henrietta slowly. 'If that happened, they would have descended on us and complained loudly. That is what they are like,' she said seriously, as though explaining the customs of some strange aboriginal tribe.

'Could go to a boozing ken and find out,' said Esau suddenly.

'I beg your pardon?' said Henrietta.

She waited patiently while Esau worked out a translation in his head. Esau had talked nothing but cant all his young life. He was trying hard to learn the King's English and was having as much difficulty with it as a foreigner.

'I shall go to a pub where the flash servants hang out,' he said carefully, 'and ask questions.'

'Splendid!' said Henrietta. 'Miss Hissop,

44

give Esau a few shillings."

'He should not be encouraged to go *drinking,*' said Miss Hissop stiffly.

'I'll only drink shrub,' said Esau. Shrub was fruit cordial mixed with rum.

'Only one glass, then,' said Miss Hissop, counting out the money.

'Give him two shillings, Miss Hissop,' said Henrietta. 'If he wishes to get information, he may have to buy a servant some beer.'

Esau took the money and went out into the cold, blustery evening.

He had a fund of underworld gossip and knew in which pubs to find the upper-class servants, since those hostelries were often frequented by thieves looking for information on how to break into some noble's house and steal the silver.

He was gone over an hour. Henrietta heard him returning, the boy's swift, light steps coming running along the street from Piccadilly. Esau never walked.

She went to the door and let him in.

'I found out, mum,' he said triumphantly. He started on a long story. Henrietta had to take him back over it time after time to iron out all the cant phrases so that she could understand. At last she had it all.

'Only peasants go to Bascombe's,' the upper

45

servants had told Esau.

'Why?' Esau had asked, and had kept on asking until it had come out that that was what the Earl of Carrisdowne was saying, and what the earl said was law.

'Oh, dear,' said Miss Hissop, when Henrietta repeated Esau's story. 'You know, Lord Charles is the earl's younger brother, and he has been paying a lot of attention to Charlotte. This must be the earl's way of trying to put us out of business.'

'But did you not say that Lady Sarah is his sister? She still sends a servant for cakes.'

'Fat as a pig,' said Esau suddenly. 'Earl don't like that neither.'

'It *must* be to put us out of business,' frowned Henrietta. 'This earl has not been here himself. He probably disapproves of Lord Charles's visits.'

'Not 'arf,' said Esau. 'Nor Mr Clifford's neither.'

'But what has Mr Clifford to do with the Earl of Carrisdowne?'

'Chums,' said Esau. 'Close as inkle weavers, they is. Carrisdowne said t'other night...' here Esau's voice rose to the strangled falsetto he considered upper-class, ' "Any fellow going to Bascombe's is indeed *making a cake of himself.*" '

46

'Is this earl so powerful?' marvelled Henrietta.

''Oh, yes,' said Josephine sadly. Josephine picked up a great deal of gossip from the lady customers. 'All the debutantes talk of little else. He is the catch of the coming Season. Rich, handsome, titled. The ladies say he looks deliciously like the wicked earl in a circulating library romance—all dark and overbearing.'

'He is a monster,' said Henrietta. 'He must have so much money, and we have so little. Why cannot he leave us alone?'

'Lord Persham's underfootman told me real ladies don't work in shops,' said Esau. 'I drew 'is cork—may the good Lord forgive me,' he added piously.

'You did the right thing,' said Henrietta firmly. 'But it is Lord Carrisdowne who should have his nose punched. Do you know, Esau, I am beginning to understand every word you say.'

'I knew I could talk flash if I put me brainbox to it,' said Esau proudly.

'Then, that is that,' said Charlotte, her eyes filling with tears.

Josephine began to cry as well. 'I h-have never m-met anyone as n-nice and *kind* as Mr Clifford before,' she sobbed. 'Now all I have left is a future of being beaten day and night by my papa. And I shall n-never s-see Mr C-Clifford *again*.'

'Fustian,' said Henrietta. 'What we need is someone more powerful than the Earl of Carrisdowne to bring us *back* into fashion. There is the Prince Regent.'

'No one seems to follow the Prince Regent, not when it comes to fashion,' said Charlotte, drying her eyes. 'Mr Brummell is still the leader. No one talks about anyone else but Brummel and Carrisdowne. But I believe he is harder to reach than the Prince Regent.'

'Of *course*,' breathed Henrietta. The fame of the great dandy had reached even the village of Partlett. Beau Brummell was an intimate of the Prince Regent. He had changed fashion by introducing impeccably tailored clothes, clean linen, and starch—'plenty of it.' Although the Beau himself was reported to be a miracle of understated elegance, most of his followers overdid his advice. Sometimes young men wore their neckcloths so high, and stiffened with so much starch, that the wearers could not turn their heads.

One young man was reported to have turned up at a dinner so starched that when he wanted to speak to the footman standing behind him he had to bend his head back until his face was horizontal. Another young man burned his chin by trying to iron the bows of his neckcloth after it was tied.

'I have an idea...I think,' said Henrietta cautiously. 'I must find out what Mr Brummell looks like. Where does he live?'

'I'll find out, miss,' said Esau, pulling his forelock.

Again he disappeared into the night, while Henrietta and the other ladies grimly set to work, trying to preserve as many of the day's uneaten delicacies as they could.

After only half an hour, Esau was back. 'Mr Brummell lives at 13 Chapel Street, which is just at Park Lane, off a South Audley Street, just a few streets away, miss.'

'Good,' said Henrietta.

'What do you plan to do?' asked Charlotte.

'I shall tell you after I have had a look at this famous Beau,' said Henrietta, 'but let me tell you one thing, Charlotte and Josephine. You may dry your tears, for Bascombe's *is not* going to fail!'

Henrietta had learned quickly that the ton did not keep country hours. The gentlemen who crept into Bascombe's at ten in the morning for their elixir were usually going home.

So at two o'clock the following afternoon, on a freezing day with the metallic smell of approaching snow in the air, Henrietta set out to walk to Chapel Street, a sketch pad under her arm.

The wind beat against her thin cloak and set it flapping about her ankles. When she got to Chapel Street, she was forced to keep walking up and down at a brisk pace, not only to keep warm, but to stop drawing any gentleman's attention to her.

Any woman strolling about at a leisurely pace, unescorted, was bound to be taken for a prostitute. She wished she had brought Esau with her.

How would she recognize the famous Beau, he who had evidently said that if people turned to stare at you in the street, then you were badly overdressed?

Just as she was about to give up, for flakes of snow were beginning to fall, she saw a slim young man emerge from Number 13. Two giggling debutantes, passing by with their maids in attendance, cried, 'Only look! There is Mr Brummell!'

Henrietta, now stationed on the opposite side of the street, whipped out her sketch pad and began to draw rapidly.

Almost as if he had noticed her and was gratified at the attention, the Beau posed on the steps of his house slowly pulling on his gloves.

He was wearing a blue swallowtail coat, tailored by the famous Weston, over a fifteen-guinea waistcoat from Guthrie's. His pantaloons were buff-coloured and tucked into glossy Hessian boots. Gentlemen were beginning to adopt pantaloons because 'Napoleon and his upstarts' had adopted breeches. He had a high-crowned beaver hat on his head of light-brown curls. His face was humorous, the nose flattened and upturned, the result of a horse having kicked it.

While Henrietta sketched busily, he finished drawing on his gloves and strolled into South Audley Street, his toes turned outward as he walked, evidently heading for St James's.

Henrietta closed her sketch pad with a sigh. Her plan *must* work.

After the confectioner's had closed that evening and the chores had been done, Henrietta set to work in the kitchen with the sketch pad beside her.

Charlotte and Josephine were curious as to what she was planning, but Henrietta sent them all to bed, saying she would need as much help as she could get on the morrow, for they were shortly to be fashionable again.

When they all appeared in the kitchen for breakfast at six in the morning, it was to find Henrietta asleep with her head on the table. In

51

front of her stood a foot and half high statuette of Beau Brummell, made out of spun sugar and coloured with vegetable dye. They circled around it in awed silence. It was, they were sure, Beau Brummell to the life. They knew that Henrietta had gone out to sketch him, but not that she meant to create confection from that hurried drawing.

Even the Beau's eyes sparkled where Henrietta had placed a coarse grain of sugar near the centre of each pupil to catch the light. His cravat of white sugar was as delicately sculptured as the original.

Henrietta stretched sleepily and yawned, and then grinned up at the circle of admiring faces.

'It is wonderful,' said Miss Hissop. 'I knew you were a good artist, Henrietta. I never realized to this moment that you were a *genius*!'

'Are you going to display it in the window?' asked Charlotte.

'No,' said Henrietta. 'Esau's new livery arrives today. He is to be washed and brushed and then he will take it to Mr Brummell as a *present.*'

Esau was so excited at the idea of his new livery that he even submitted to taking a wash in a tin bath in the kitchen behind a sheet pinned up as a screen.

He privately thought the whole business of

bathing was shameful and indecent and had anyone other than Henrietta told him to scrub himself, he would most definitely have refused.

But Henrietta's soft voice and large brown eyes, which smiled on him in such a merry way, had done more for poor Esau than any workhouse whippings. What Miss Henrietta wanted, Miss Henrietta should have. The bathwater was scented with rose petals, and Esau began to find the novelty of washing quite pleasant.

Miss Hissop thought Henrietta had gone too far by insisting the boy wash himself all over. But Miss Hissop had to admit to herself that Henrietta had very odd notions when it came to washing and even soaped and washed her own hair, which everyone knew could lead to all sorts of agues and fevers.

Dressed in his best and looking even more sinister with his hair powdered—it seemed to accentuate his squint—Esau set out.

He came back quite crestfallen. He had hoped to have presented it to the Beau himself, but Mr Brummell's servant had simply taken the large beribboned box and told Esau rudely to 'hop it.'

Although Beau Brummell's household effects boasted a dinner service of twelve oval dishes, twenty soup plates, and seventy-eight meat plates, as well as nine wine coolers, three claret jugs, a dozen hock glasses, and forty others, Mr Brummell usually dined out at friends' houses.

But that very evening he was holding one of his rare dinner parties. Henrietta's statue was not exhibited on his dining table, but on a special stand placed in the middle of his chintz-upholstered, Brussells-carpeted drawing room upstairs where he received his guests.

Candles had been arranged to set the grains of sugar in the candy eyes sparkling to perfection. His guests exclaimed, admired, and all began to gossip about Bascombe's. 'Who is saying it is a common establishment?' asked Mr Brummell crossly. 'In my opinion, it is the home of a genius. And you say Bascombe is not some ancient pastry cook but a pretty, genteel lady?'

'Carrisdowne says no one who's anyone goes there,' was the reply from all sides.

Mr Brummell said gently. 'When could Carrisdowne—such a stiff soldier one expects him to wear a cannonball in his stickpin—*when* could our military friend ever appreciate the finer things of life, whether a painting, a pretty ankle, or...' he waved his quizzing glass at the statue '...a work of genius?'

Mr Brummell had only a nodding acquaintance with the earl. But he was vastly annoyed that society should follow anyone else's dictates.

'I have heard that he is a bully, horse-whipping sort of fellow,' went on Mr Brummell. 'Oh, he is a fine figure of a man and dresses almost as well as I myself. But he has such a *badly dressed mind.*'

'Such a badly dressed mind,' muttered everyone gleefully, saving those bon mots to pass around at less exalted gatherings.

'Now Gunter's,' went on the Beau pensively, 'has become quite dull. I actually brushed shoulders with a merchant there the other day, and had to ask my valet to throw the besmirched coat away.'

Mr Brummell's views could not damn socially such a marriageable man as the Earl of Carrisdowne. But they could, and did, bring Bascombe's roaring back into fashion.

By the end of another week, Henrietta had the pleasure of being able to save a daily table for Mr Clifford and Lord Charles, who had arrived back in London and to employ three kitchen maids.

The Duchess of Gillingham renewed her order for a centrepiece. Henrietta sent her 'Hannibal Crossing the Alps,' taken from

Turner's famous painting, which had just been exhibited at the Royal Academy. Marzipan elephants strained up sugar mountains, laden with baskets of tiny sweetmeats wrapped in gold and silver foil.

Bascombe's appeared for the first time in the social column of the *Times*.

Mr Clifford, grown courageous, laughed in the Earl of Carrisdowne's face and accused him of behaving like a Methodist. 'Imagine,' said Mr Clifford, 'what a figure of fun you look trying to stop your brother and your best friend from visiting a respectable confectioner's in the middle of the afternoon. You have a badly dressed mind.'

'So I keep hearing,' said the earl dryly. 'It seems I am become an ogre even to my best friend.'

Mr Clifford blushed. 'It ain't that I'm not grateful to you for all the messes you've pulled me out of in the past, Rupert, it just seems terribly stuffy to go on like a Dutch uncle over an innocent taking of tea. When did you ever think it odd to look at pretty girls?'

'Never,' grinned the earl. 'What has made this Bascombe's so violently popular again?'

'Haven't you heard? Little Miss Bascombe sent a statuette of Brummell to him, made out of sugar, the most wonderful thing anyone has ever seen.'

'Clever of her,' said the earl thoughtfully. 'Very clever.'

'Why don't you have a look at the place for yourself,' said Mr Clifford eagerly. 'I know what it is—you're worried about Sarah stuffing her face with cakes. You're not really worried about Charles or me. It's not as if we aren't old enough to look after ourselves. But Sarah has always had a terribly sweet tooth, and if you forbid her to either go or send the servants to Bascombe's, she'll simply go back to Gunter's. Besides, you can't stop anyone eating these days. There's such a monstrous deal of food around.'

'For those that can afford it,' said the earl. 'And those that can could exist on a fraction of what they eat. Someone who shared dinner-for two at Lord Stafford's told me they dined on soup, fish, fricassee of chicken, cutlets, venison, veal, hare, vegetables of all kinds, tart, melon, pineapple, grapes, peaches and nectarines, and with six servants to wait on the two of them.

'But I shall certainly call on Bascombe's Guy. It is ridiculous of me to damn a place I have never set foot in.'

The earl appeared at Bascombe's just before

closing time. He had decided that his fears were groundless and that the ladies there would prove to be quite ordinary shopgirls pretending to be duchesses.

He ordered turtle soup and sat at a small table and looked at Henrietta, Charlotte and Josephine with a sinking heart. They were each of them beautiful in quite a different way. They were undoubtedly ladies by birth, although their present occupation had certainly reduced them to the ranks of the demimonde. But the earl knew how terribly susceptible his younger brother and best friend were. Beauty decked out in domestic aprons and surrounded by food. The combination was hellishly seductive.

Henrietta studied her customer curiously. He was drinking his soup as though it were poison. She decided he was by far the most attractive man she had ever seen since she had come to London. The exquisites were too feminine, the masculine members of the Corinthian set too brutish in their sports and manners.

This gentleman, mused Henrietta, looked powerful and strong, and yet there was a certain sensitivity in his harsh face and drooping eyelids. He glanced up and caught her staring at him, and looked steadily back, his black, black eyes giving nothing away. Henrietta stood rigid, one hand on the counter of the shop, feeling as shaken as if he had tried to assault her.

Josephine passed close to her with a tray of confectionery. 'One of the ladies who has just left,' she murmured in Henrietta's ear, 'said that *that* over there, eating soup, is none other than our enemy, the Earl of Carrisdowne.'

'Oh,' said Henrietta weakly. 'He is not at all what I expected.'

She had built up in her mind a picture of a middle-aged tyrant with a brutal face—despite the fact that the lady customers had said he was handsome. Anyone with a title and a fortune was vowed handsome, that much Henrietta had learned very quickly.

Since six in the evening was now the regular hour for closing, by ten to six the last of the customers had collected hats and canes, shawls and reticules, and were making their way out. Still the earl stayed.

Charlotte was the next to flutter up. 'That is Carrisdowne,' she whispered, and when Henrietta nodded, added, 'Why does he not *go?*'

'Because I think he wishes to speak to me,' said Henrietta. She was now calm. The earl was a man like any other. He had a great deal of power but fortunately not more than Mr Brummell.

59

'Get Miss Hissop and Josephine, and stay in the back shop with Esau until I call you,' muttered Henrietta. 'I can handle this better alone.'

The earl sat listening to the hissings and mutterings as the ladies tried to stay while Henrietta shooed them all into the back shop.

Then she walked to the door and drew down the blind and, turning to the earl, said sweetly, 'We are now closed, sir. I do not wish to hurry you, but as you have finished your soup...'

The earl's black eyes locked with Henrietta's brown ones. 'I stayed quite deliberately, madam,' he said. 'I have something to say to you.'

Henrietta unpinned her apron and folded it neatly on the counter. Then she unpinned her frivolous cap with the jaunty streamers. She would face this adversary as a lady, not as a shopgirl.

She sat down opposite the earl. 'Very well, Lord Carrisdowne,' said Henrietta Bascombe. 'What is it you wish to say?'

CHAPTER FOUR

The earl looked thoughtfully at Henrietta's flushed face and bright eyes.

'I shall speak to you plain, Miss Bascombe. My brother, Lord Charles Worsley, and my friend, Mr Clifford, are frequent customers here.'

Henrietta nodded. 'They come every day when they are in town.'

'Delicious as your confections appear to be, I am persuaded that the attraction is either yourself or the two other ladies who work for you..'

'Indeed?' Henrietta tilted her little chin defiantly.

'Yes, indeed. Both Mr Clifford and my brother are gullible young men.'

'I would not call Mr Clifford exactly *young*,' interrupted Henrietta.

'How old are you?'

'Nineteen,' said Henrietta.

'Mr Clifford is twenty-nine but is young for his years. Charles is twenty-three. I have rescued both in the past from unsuitable alliances—an opera dancer and a member of the fashionable impure, to be precise.'

'Since no one here belongs to either set, I do not see—'

'Madam, I wish you to repel any advances these two men might make to you or your companions, or it will be the worse for you,' grated the earl.

'How *dare* you!' raged Henrietta. 'We are all *ladies*.'

'It seems to me,' he said calmly, 'that you *were* all ladies at one time. But not now. Ladies do not go into trade.'

'Let me tell you, my fine buck,' said Henrietta, 'that I do not consider *you* a gentleman. Making malicious remarks to stop society from coming here. What on earth do you have against four poor women trying to make a living?'

'Women such as yourself, whom the good Lord has seen fit to place among the gentry, do not work. They marry.'

'Pooh,' said Henrietta. 'I do not wish to get married. I am much better off as I am.'

'You...do...not...wish...to...get...married?' The earl looked dumbfounded. There had been an unmistakable ring of truth in her voice.

'No.'

He looked at her shrewdly. 'And your female

assistants. Do they feel the same?'

Henrietta bit her lip. The truth was that despite her desire to turn Charlotte and Josephine into businesswomen, she knew that in their hearts of hearts they were ashamed of being in trade and had their lives back in Partlett not been so thoroughly nasty, they would have returned on the first available stage.

'They are as competent as myself when it comes to making their own way,' she said. 'Tell me, my lord, I can understand you forbidding your younger brother to go anywhere of which you disapprove. It amazes me, however, that you should be able to command Mr Clifford.'

'I do not *command* my friend to do anything. I merely suggest—'

'And tag on a warning.'

'No. I merely point out the obvious. You have all gone into trade, and therefore you are none of you marriageable.'

'Let me tell you, my lord, that somehow, somewhere, there must be a man who does not care—who would be *proud* of us. We have proved that gently bred ladies can earn their wages.'

He rose to his feet. 'Let me know when you find him, Miss Bascombe. I have never yet met a saint.'

'Oh, do not rush off,' said Henrietta sweetly,

'without telling me what you will do should I not carry out your wish regarding your brother and friend.'

'If either my brother or Mr Clifford should be so addlepated as to propose to one of you and be accepted, then I shall...I shall—'

'Yes, my lord?'

'Damn you, madam, I shall be very angry indeed!'

Henrietta's enchanting trill of laughter followed him out into the street. He marched to the corner of Half Moon Street and Piccadilly and stopped. He turned and looked back.

It had been snowing lightly that day, a fresh fall. The warm lights from the confectioner's shone a welcome into the cold street. The golden pineapple above the door swung in the wind.

He felt an odd mixture of fury and exultation. She had had the better of him, but By George he was looking forward to the forthcoming battle! But what on earth could he do to them now that they enjoyed the patronage of Mr Brummell?

Every woman had her price, the earl thought cynically. Imagine any woman declaring—and meaning it—that she had no interest in marriage.

Although he had not yet met any woman who

had found enough favour in his eyes to make him want to take her as wife, he was well aware that, for their part, the ladies fell before him like ninepins. He had not been back in London a week before they were up to every plot and plan to catch his attention. But cynical acquaintances were quick to point out that his title and fortune were the attraction. And I imagined it was because I might be perhaps as handsome as they claim I am, the earl had thought gloomily.

'Miss Bascombe has now made me feel that *she*, at least, would not take me under any terms,' he muttered to himself.

He walked up Piccadilly past the Green Park, still deep in thought, with a bright little picture of Henrietta, all flushed face, bright eyes, and heaving bosom, dancing before his eyes.

Suppose...just suppose he made Miss Bascombe fall in love with him...She was the owner and the driving force behind the business. Were she in love with him, she would gladly go for walks and drives with him, and the business would falter and die. By the time she discovered he really had no interest in her at all, other than keeping her and her assistants away from his brother and friend, it would be too late.

He had never *tried* to make a woman fall in

love with him before. But it should be quite easy. Women had nothing else in their heads but fashions and flowers, beaux and romances.

Yes, definitely a challenge. And by pretending to court Henrietta, he could visit the shop often and make sure Guy and Charles were behaving themselves.

Something also, would have to be done about Sarah. Although he was quite good at disciplining Charles, he had never been able to do anything with Sarah. His face cleared. His mother, the Dowager Countess of Carrisdowne, who had been taking the waters at Bath, had written only that day to say she was much improved.

Very well. Sarah should be sent to Bath. Instead of making her come-out at the Season in London, she could make her debut at the famous spa. It would not matter if nothing came of it. She was still very young. But Mama would see to it that she kept away from treacherous confectioners and their devilish wares.

The problem of Sarah having been dealt with, the earl turned his mind once more to Miss Bascombe. He enjoyed thinking about her. She was such a defiant little miss. It would be enjoyable to bring her down a peg. He could hardly wait to begin.

'And,' ended Henrietta, looking around the kitchen, 'do you know what his terrible threat was? He threatened to become very angry with me.' She laughed and laughed, until she realized no one was joining in.

The kitchen maids had returned to their homes, and Henrietta was seated at the kitchen table surrounded by Charlotte, Josephine, Miss Hissop and Esau.

'What is the matter?' she cried. 'There is nothing to be afraid of. He can't do anything to Bascombe's.'

'No,' said Charlotte sadly. She stood up and kissed Henrietta on the cheek. 'And now you must excuse me. I am so very tired and shall feel better for an early night.'

'I, too,' said Josephine, trailing out after her.

'Going out for a bit, mum,' said Esau, sidling out the back door.

Henrietta looked in amazement at Miss Hissop. 'What is wrong with them? I *told* them the wicked earl cannot do anything to Bascombe's.'

'I think he can, however, make sure that Mr Clifford and Lord Charles do not marry either of them,' said Miss Hissop quietly.

'Oh.' Henrietta put her hands up to her hot cheeks. 'I was feeling so triumphant at having got the best of him that I quite forgot. Bascombe's means so very much to me. But alas for Josephine and Charlotte. All they want to do is fall in love and get married. It is most odd of them.'

'Henrietta,' cried Miss Hissop. 'I beg of you...you are not talking sense, you know. What is it all for? The Season and the gowns and the duennas? Almack's, the Italian opera, the routs, the fetes, the breakfasts? Why...so that John may marry Jill! There is *no other future for a lady!* If she does not marry, and the family is not rich, then she may be lucky enough to find a post as a companion...or governess.

'Have you not considered my plight? We are making a great deal of money, but we also spend a great deal creating novelties. Flour is a wicked expense. What if we lose all? And I...poor Miss Hissop...am buried in a pauper's grave? Have you no feelings? Why not be done and give my poor old body to the anatomists at St George's Hospital? Oh, lovely black horses and weeping mutes where are you now? Gone. Alas, all gone.'

'If only I were a man, the Carrisdownes of this world would not plague me so,' said Henrietta. 'Please, do not distress yourself. We are all so tired. So very tired. You may stay in bed tomorrow, all day long, and rest.'

'No,' said Miss Hissop, striking her scrawny bosom with her fist. 'I shall see it through. When Bascombe's lies at my feet in ashes and ruins, I shall say *hah* to the Fates.'

'Go and say *hah* to your pillow, my good friend,' said Henrietta gently. Miss Hissop was behaving so oddly and so...well, insanely...that her conscience was smiting her. She should never have persuaded this timid spinster into coming to London.

Had the shrewd Earl of Carrisdowne been there, perhaps he might have told Miss Bascombe that Miss Hissop was enjoying her dramatics immensely. But he was not, and so Henrietta led her old friend upstairs to the dormitory, waited until she had undressed, and then tucked her into bed as if she were a child.

'Do not worry about a thing, dear Ismene,' she said, kissing a worn cheek. Henrietta had never called Miss Hissop by her first name before, but the older woman now appeared to her as defenceless as a child.

Henrietta quietly blew out the candle beside Miss Hissop's bed and left the room—but not before she had heard a stifled sob from Charlotte's bed.

'Should I have left them all behind?' anguished Henrietta to herself. 'But Josephine might have been beaten to death by now, and Charlotte might have died of cold or starvation, or both.'

Then she thought of the earl. Somehow, things would work out. She would *make* them work out. If only for the pleasure of showing the earl that he could not stop her.

Why, oh *why*, had Josephine and Charlotte had to fall in love so soon? Henrietta had planned to amass a fortune and then persuade Miss Hissop to take them all to Bath and chaperon them at the assemblies. They would be respectable again by that time and with large dowries. Henrietta did not plan to find a husband for herself. She had only dreamed of the pleasure of seeing Josephine and Charlotte comfortably settled.

She tidied up the remaining dishes in the kitchen and washed out the sticky metal trays.

Water was supplied to the shop—as it was supplied to all the houses of the West End—only twice a day, and then it had to be pumped up into a cistern on the roof. It was one of Esau's many chores.

Esau. Esau, too, would need to be taken care of. He must never return to the workhouse.

Feeling suddenly exhausted, Henrietta went out into the street and paid the night watchman sixpence so that he might shout extra loudly outside their shop at six in the morning and wake them up.

The next day they were as busy as ever, and each had little time to worry about personal matters. Mr Clifford and Lord Charles were, however, upset to find that neither Josephine nor Charlotte had a smile for them.

Lord Charles and Mr Clifford finally took their leave and walked along the street, arm in arm.

'Not so jolly there today,' remarked Lord Charles casually. 'Pretty widow, Mrs Webster. Don't like to see her so quiet and withdrawn.'

'Miss Archer didn't even look at me,' said Mr Clifford, tossing a coin to a crossing sweeper. They gloomily picked their way across Half Moon Street and into Curzon Street.

'Tell you what it is,' said Lord Charles. 'I think Rupert's behind this. Think he's scared 'em off.'

'Think you're right,' said Mr Clifford.

'By George,' said Lord Charles, 'I wish I could handle him like Sarah. She ups this morning and tells him he's a horrible martinet, has no soul, no feeling, and is nothing more than a piece of cannon fodder in dandy's clothing.'

'Did he whip her?' asked Mr Clifford with interest.

'Not he. Wouldn't strike any woman,

71

especially not his own sister,' said Lord Charles. 'He'd told her she was to go to Mama in Bath and drink the waters and forsake the confectioners, so she ripped up at him.'

'But she went, didn't she?' asked Mr Clifford.

'Yes.'

'Well, ain't that what always happens? He always gets his way.'

'But, dash it all, she's only seventeen and has been summoned by Mama as well as being bundled off by Rupert. Not the same as me.'

'Isn't it?' said Mr Clifford, giving him a sidelong look. 'I think Rupert will be more circumspect if he wants to spike my guns this time. Trouble is, the man ain't ever been in love.'

'And are you?' asked Lord Charles anxiously.

'Yes. Yes, I am. Very much so. Right up to the neck in love.'

'Not...not...Mrs Webster?' asked Lord Charles.

'Who? Oh, *her*. No, of course not. T'other one. Miss Archer.'

'Let me shake your hand,' cried Lord Charles, 'and wish you luck.'

'No need to be so violent. It's a hand, not a pump handle. Oh, I say, you ain't spoony about Mrs Webster?'

'Love her madly,' said Lord Charles. 'Terribly, awfully, madly.'

A cloud of worry once more dampened Mr Clifford's high spirits. 'I'll help you if you help me,' he said. 'But it's going to be deuced awkward. If only Rupert would fall in love. *Then* he would know what it's all about!'

'If only Henrietta would fall in love,' muttered Josephine to Charlotte as they loaded confections onto trays in the back shop of Bascombe's. 'Then she might understand our misery.'

Charlotte sighed and brushed a strand of black hair from her hot forehead. 'I think Henrietta loves confectionery and nothing else. What's more, I don't think she ever will.'

'Well, it's nearly closing time, and it's Saturday,' said Josephine. 'Lovely Sunday. I shall sleep all day, and Henrietta can pay my shilling fine for not going to church.'

She opened the door to the shop with her shoulder, saw the gentleman who was just entering, and swung back into the kitchen again. 'It's Carrisdowne!' she said.

'What does he want?' squeaked Charlotte.

'I do not know. Let me put this tray down.' Josephine opened the door and peered round it. 'He is saying something to Henrietta. He is standing very close to her and whispering something.'

'Threats?'

'No, she is smiling. She is shaking hands with him. He has ordered something and is taking a table. Oh, Charlotte. Perhaps everything is going to be all right after all.'

Inside the shop, Henrietta busily served customers and wondered what had come over the Earl of Carrisdowne.

Her first thought when she saw his tall figure was that he had come to make trouble. But he had bent his handsome head very near to her own, so near that his breath had fanned her cheek, and had said in a low voice, 'I am come to apologize for my boorish behaviour. Please say you forgive me.' And then he had smiled into her eyes. Henrietta, feeling weak at the knees, had taken his proffered hand and mumbled that, yes, she forgave him.

He ordered a portion of orange salad and then, after greeting various acquaintances, went and sat down.

Henrietta nervously spooned the salad into a small glass dish. She had made it from oranges, muscatel raisins, brandy, and pounded sugar. She placed it in front of him, bobbed a curtsy, and would have left, but he looked about him as if searching for a topic of conversation. 'Stay a moment,' he said. 'Tell me, why do you not have ices?'

'Perhaps I might begin to make ices in a small way,' said Henrietta. 'I have not even tried, because I am always aware of the great competition from Gunter's. *They* ship their ice from Greenland. I could perhaps buy ice in London and the machinery to make ices—but the equipment costs a great deal of money, so perhaps I shall wait a little longer until my finances are more secure.'

The earl looked around the busy little shop. 'I should have said they were very secure already.'

'Not quite. People are ordering elaborate centrepieces for their tables. What if...' Henrietta paused. She had been about to say. 'What if we should become unfashionable again?'

She said instead, 'What if they cancel their orders? Even just one cancelled order would mean a loss of money. I shall go carefully for the moment.'

'Very wise.' Again the earl smiled at her. 'You do not work on Sundays?'

'Of course not,' said Henrietta. She blushed at the lie, for she knew that Sunday was the day she went over the accounts, but even in

75

this godless age, the earl might find that rather shocking.

'I go to church, of course,' she added quickly.

'Then, in that case I should consider myself honoured if you would allow me to escort you. Do you go to St George's?'

Henrietta shook her head. 'Grosvenor Chapel.'

'And may I have your company?'

A customer behind Henrietta rapped angrily on the table with his fork for service. 'I shall return in a moment, my lord,' she said.

As she busily attended to the needs of the other customers, Henrietta thought quickly. The earl's presence in Bascombe's, after all he had said about it, was occasioning pleased surprise and comment from the other customers. It would do no harm to encourage the earl. And what could be more respectable than attending church with him.

When there was a lull, she returned to his table. 'I am most grateful to you, my lord,' she said. 'I shall accept your escort. Do you mind escorting Miss Hissop as well? She never misses church service.'

'By all means, Miss Hissop, too,' he said, rising to his feet. He paid for his salad, made Henrietta a magnificent bow, and left.

Henrietta could hardly wait for the shop to

close so that she could discuss this new development with the others.

Charlotte and Josephine were delighted. Esau said nothing, but he was privately worried. It would be just like a beauty like Miss Henrietta to go and get married, he thought. And then what would become of poor Esau? The horrors of the workhouse rose before his eyes. He remembered being subjected to blows, starvation, and putrid air, the lice, itch, and filth, and always surrounded by the plaintive cries of the dying. He ran a hand down the soft plush of his livery.

Henrietta *must* not marry. He had overheard her saying she did not want to.

Miss Hissop voiced her disapproval. 'Dear child,' she exclaimed, 'dear Henrietta. Only consider. Man in Carrisdowne's position... don't mean anything respectable. Ah, I see it now. The silks, the jewels, the apartment in Jermyn Street, the villa in Kensington...then, "You weary me, Miss Bascombe, I shall pass you on to Sir Evil Nasty"...then cheaper addresses and muslin, no carriage, one maid... then passed down to a merchant...then crying for shillings at the opera. Oh, my doomed child!'

Henrietta looked at Miss Hissop in exasperation. 'I am not going to fall in love with the earl,

Miss Hissop—only *use* him. Now that even *he* has been seen at Bascombe's means assured success for us.

'And Charlotte and Josephine, I know you have formed certain *tendres* for Lord Charles and Mr Clifford, but that is because you have not been in the way of meeting a *variety* of gentlemen.'

'Many gentlemen come to the confectioner's,' said Charlotte stiffly. 'Lord Charles and Mr Clifford are the only two who treat us as ladies. The others treat us simply as shopgirls, and once they find out we are not interested in a dubious relationship with them, then they confine their interest to sweetmeats and leave us alone.'

'But listen!' cried Henrietta. 'I have never outlined my plans for you and Josephine. If we make a great deal of money during the Season, then we shall go to Bath or some other fashionable watering spa and, with dowries apiece, we shall be able to *choose* husbands.'

'I thought *you* were not interested in marriage,' snapped Josephine.

'Not for myself. But for the both of you,' pleaded Henrietta. 'Only give it a little time. Do you know'—she rested her chin on her hands and looked round at them with sparkling eyes—'it will be interesting to see if I can

78

make the great Earl of Carrisdowne fall in love with me.'

Josephine and Charlotte exchanged glances. If only Henrietta herself would fall in love. *Then* she might not be so insensitive to their plight!

CHAPTER FIVE

For most of London society, Sunday was a boring twenty-four hours stretching between one gambling session and the next. Never had gambling fever been so great. Both men and women of society spent long hours at the tables.

Although Methodism and Evangelism flourished among the lesser breeds, the ton politely suffered God and all his angels on this one day of the week. There was a general uneasy feeling that religion had no place among the top ten thousand. It was enough that God had placed them in their exalted stations. They would much rather have gone on enjoying being exalted without the labour of sitting in a cold church, praying fervently for the service to end.

Henrietta was unfashionable enough to enjoy her weekly visits to church. She always left after the service feeling refreshed and with courage to face the week ahead once more renewed.

Josephine and Charlotte, however, had decided to stay in bed. They envied Henrietta and her stamina. Despite the new addition to the staff of three daily kitchen maids, they found the long weeks of work beginning to take their toll.

Josephine had sleepily told Henrietta to help herself from her wardrobe. Josephine had the most fashionable clothes of the three girls. Determined to enchant the earl, Henrietta cheerfully selected one of Josephine's best day ensembles.

It was a promenade dress consisting of a Spanish pelisse of white-and-lilac shot sarcenet, trimmed with Chinese scalloped binding, and worn over a white muslin gown. On her head she wore a woodland hat of lemon-coloured chip straw, decorated with a curled ostrich feather of lilac and white. She was drawing on a pair of lemon-coloured kid gloves and peering through the shop window for a sight of the earl's coach when Miss Hissop came down to join her.

Miss Hissop had, for the moment, forgotten her distrust of Lord Carrisdowne's intentions and was happily excited at the idea of making her entrance in chuṛch on the arm of a member of the nobility. She was wearing a purple velvet walking dress, and on her head she wore a large black-velvet turban. Henrietta noted that Miss Hissop's own gown was sadly 'seated' at the back where the velvet had grown shiny with age, and she was about to urge her to borrow one of Josephine's shawls when the earl suddenly arrived. A quick glance out of the window showed no coach outside, and she realized with surprise that the earl had come on foot.

He offered an arm to each. He was in morning dress, the plated buttons of his coat of Bath superfine winking in the pale sunlight.

The day was very cold. The snow had melted during the night and had then frozen during the morning. As they walked along, Henrietta shivered miserably and wondered how on earth she had ever been stupid enough to think she could attract such a man as the Earl of Carrisdowne.

As they turned along Curzon Street in the direction of South Audley Street, Henrietta looked at the other ladies heading in the direction of the church. Some were attired in thinner clothing than herself, muslins fluttering in the biting wind.

'I shall never follow the dictates of fashion

again—not on a cold day, at least,' said Henrietta.

The tall earl smiled down at her. 'There is a tinge of lilac in your cheeks that matches the colour of your pelisse.'

'Meaning I am blue with cold,' said Henrietta crossly.

He turned and raised his hand. His footman, whom Henrietta had not noticed, had been following some distance behind. The earl stepped aside and said a few words to him, and the servant hurried off.

Miss Hissop, who had been silent up till then, decided the time had come to show the earl that dear Henrietta had a protector. 'I am surprised,' she said, 'to hear you talking thus about fashion on the Sunday morn, Henrietta. You usually have a mind above such petty things. Henrietta,' she added, fixing the earl with a basilisk stare, 'is *very* devout.'

The earl nodded politely.

'We *never* miss church on Sundays,' went on Miss Hissop. 'Never. We go in the rain, the sleet, the snow, and the scorching days of summer. *Always.*'

'Miss Hissop,' said Henrietta in stifled tones, 'I am sure my lord does not wish a sermon *before* he gets to church.'

'But you know it is true,' expostulated Miss

Hissop. 'I feel it is the only place—church, that is—where a young maiden is free from the perils of this loose and decadent society!'

As they reached the steps of Grosvenor Chapel, a pleasant little church built in 1730, the earl's servant came hurrying up with a huge fur cape over his arm. The earl took it from him and put it around Henrietta's shoulders. Henrietta felt she should protest, for several members of the ton were staring at them with open curiosity, but the warmth of the fur was so wonderful that she merely murmured her thanks.

Henrietta had forgotten that no one was equal in this house of the Lord. The rich had their pews near the pulpit. The servants and shopkeepers such as herself sat on plain benches at the back.

The Earl of Carrisdowne usually attended church service at St George's, Hanover Square. It was unthinkable that he should sit with the common folk at the rear of the church. In a whisper, Henrietta urged him to share the pew of one of his friends. But the earl replied in a low voice that, for his part, he really did not care where he sat.

Henrietta was conscious of the sensation they were causing as they sat down, although the earl appeared indifferent to it. Some of the nobility were standing up on the benches and levelling their quizzing glasses over the tops of their pews to get a better look at the Earl of Carrisdowne sitting with the common people.

'Didn't know Carrisdowne was a Jacobite,' said the Duke of Gillingham, creaking down, after a good look at the earl, to sit beside his wife.

'He's been away at the wars too long,' sniffed the duchess. 'If he wants to make that confectioner girl his mistress, then he shouldn't make a parade of the fact in church.'

Henrietta hugged the fur cape closely about her and decided to concentrate on the service. There would be no reading from the New Testament, of that she was sure. Society preferred the blood and thunder of the Old Testament, free from any nasty remarks about the rich having a hard time getting into the kingdom of heaven.

There was not much of a sermon. Even that relic of Puritanism was slowly disappearing, and the days when the sermon was the highlight of the service, to be discussed and debated afterward, had been slowly dying out.

But the feeling of content that Henrietta usually experienced in church would not come. She was very conscious of the earl as a *man*. He was very tall, very strong, and very masculine. He had removed his gloves to turn the pages of the hymnbook for her, and his hands were long-fingered and tanned, with square nails, a contrast to the hands of the other aristocrats, which where usually white-leaded on the backs to make them appear delicate, and painted pink on the palms with cochineal.

Why had he decided to be pleasant to her and seek her company? Had he some plot in mind? The more Henrietta thought about it, the more odd and out of character his apology appeared. She realized with a start that the church service was over and that she had not heard one word of it.

Miss Hissop was thoroughly embarrassed by all the attention. Like Henrietta, she had forgotten about the seating arrangements in the church. She had vaguely thought that, by his very presence, the earl would be able to conjure up a private pew.

The earl stopped outside the church to chat with various friends, all of whom were Henrietta's customers. Each time, he drew Henrietta and Miss Hissop a little forward and introduced them. But hard eyes stared insolently, and hard voices said, 'Hah, yes. Been to your shop.'

What if they think I do not know my place and will punish me by not coming to my shop? thought Henrietta miserably. Did the earl know this? Is *that* why he took me to church?'

The earl was engaged in talking about the war in the peninsula to an elderly gentleman. He half turned to introduce Henrietta and Miss Hissop, but the old gentleman caught hold of his sleeve and asked him whether the war was not as the Whigs declared, a monstrous waste of men and money.

The earl turned back, and Henrietta decided to escape. 'Come along, Miss Hissop,' she whispered.

They hurried off down the street, but the earl caught up with them as they were rounding the corner into Curzon Street. 'You should have known I meant to escort you back, Miss Bascombe,' he said severely, 'if only to get my cloak back.'

'You were engaged in conversation,' said Henrietta. She drew a deep breath. 'We occasioned too much comment by being seen in your company in the common seats, my lord.'

'You have already occasioned much comment by running a shop,' he replied, taking her arm and offering his other to Miss Hissop. 'I was under the impression you did not trouble yourself over the rules of society.'

Alarmed that, by this statement, the earl meant he considered Henrietta an immoral hoyden, Miss Hissop burst into incoherent speech. 'Not at all...dear Henrietta, *very* well brought up...would never tie her garter in public...strictly chaperoned...I did not realize my lord meant to join us at the back of the church...' and on she went until they reached the shop.

She finally ran out of breath as Henrietta opened the shop door. Swinging the cape from her shoulders, Henrietta handed it to the earl. 'Thank you, my lord,' she said. 'It was kind of you to escort me. I fear, however, I have made us both look ridiculous.'

He looked down at the dignified figure in the lilac pelisse. He saw the worry and concern in the large eyes looking so directly up into his. 'It was not to make you unfashionable again,' he said gently. 'On the contrary, those who have not yet met you will be beating a path to your door to have a look at you.'

'Nonetheless, it is all very unpleasant,' said Henrietta firmly. 'I do not wish to be such an object of curiosity. It makes me feel like one of those poor shabby animals in the Tower zoo.'

'My apologies,' he said. 'I should have taken you to St George's, where my family has a pew. Come driving with me this afternoon, Miss Bascombe. There is nothing more respectable than a drive in the park at the fashionable hour.'

'No thank you,' said Henrietta firmly. 'I have caused sufficient comment for today. Besides, I have work to do.'

'Liar,' he mocked. 'And you said you never worked on a Sunday.'

'I meant work at my prayers,' said Henrietta crossly. She curtsied to him and went into the shop and closed the door.

The earl stood with a half smile on his face. She certainly was an enchanting creature—but one who did not seem in the slightest interested in him.

He turned and walked away, signalling to his servant to take the heavy fur cape from him.

'It's just like a battle,' he thought to himself. 'The trouble is I have no real plan of campaign. First, I must earn her gratitude...'

By the next morning Henrietta was already regretting having turned down the earl's invitation to go driving in the park. Charlotte and Josephine had looked worried and anxious when she had told them. Secretly both had hoped that Mr Clifford and Lord Charles would ask *them* to go driving if they saw the Earl of Carrisdowne was not too high in the instep to be seen around with Henrietta.

Just before the shop opened, two servants dressed in the Earl of Carrisdowne's livery appeared at the shop door. They had, they said, a present for Miss Bascombe.

Henrietta looked at the huge parcel in dismay. Then the earl's intentions *were* dishonourable. This should have come neither as a surprise, nor should it have caused such a sharp pain around the region of her heart, but Henrietta was upset nonetheless. Gentlemen might send bouquets of flowers or poems to a lady they admired. Only members of the demimonde received expensive presents.

'Convey my thanks to your master and tell him I am unable to accept this,' she said, backing away from the huge box.

'Begging your pardon, miss,' said one, 'my lord told us you might say that, and said to urge you to examine the contents before you refused.'

'Very well,' said Henrietta, 'but I shall probably send it back just the same.'

With the help of the two servants, she opened the box and then looked with amazement at the contents. Never before, surely, had a gentleman sent a lady such an unromantic gift.

In the box were all the ingredients to make ices. There was a large tub big enough to hold a bushel of ice, a freezing pot made of pewter, a bright spaddle made of copper, and even a cellaret where the ices could be stored for a short time.

To Henrietta, blinking away sudden tears, it seemed as if the earl, by his gift, had declared his approval of her being in trade. She had not realized until that moment how very much she had minded the censure of society.

'Thank my lord very much,' she said. 'And tell him I am delighted to accept his gift.'

Henrietta sang to herself as she went about her work that day. Mr Clifford and Lord Charles arrived at their usual time. Josephine and Charlotte were lucky. There was a lull in business, and they were able to engage in brief conversations with the gentlemen.

But soon the little shop was busy again, and Mr Clifford and Lord Charles took their leave. Henrietta found herself glancing hopefully at the door each time the little bell above it tinkled to announce a new customer. The earl must surely come, if only to find out how she liked her gift. But by closing time there was no sign of his tall figure.

After the daily maids had cleared up, and Josephine, Charlotte, Esau, and Miss Hissop had retired to the back shop to take tea, Henrietta sat behind the counter of the shop and looked out onto Half Moon Street.

Esau appeared briefly to ask if he might put up the shutters, but Henrietta told him to leave them for the moment and sent him back to join the others.

Snow was beginning to fall gently. What a cold spring! It was now March. The Season began in April. One profitable Season might bring them their dowries, mused Henrietta. But although many of the aristocracy ordered set pieces that were expensive to prepare and took long hours to make, they seemed reluctant to pay their bills. There must be *some* way of getting them to pay, thought Henrietta, without offending them.

Her heart gave a lurch as she recognized the earl's footman, the one who had followed them to church on Sunday. He walked up the steps and rapped on the door. Henrietta ran to open it. He handed her a letter, touched his hat, and left.

Henrietta carried the letter back into the circle of candlelight and broke open the seal. The contents were brief and businesslike:

Dear Miss Bascombe,
I am giving an entertainment this Friday at my town house at 12 Upper Brook Street. I wish to order a centrepiece. The subject I shall leave to your imagination.

Carrisdowne

Well, thought Henrietta breathlessly, what else did I expect? It is a business letter to a businesswoman, nothing more.

For one moment, she felt very young and alone. It flashed through her mind that it would be wonderful to go to the earl's as a guest, not as a shopkeeper making deliveries, to return to a pleasant town house with her parents afterward, instead of back to her place of work, to be loved and cossetted, instead of having to be responsible for, love and cosset her companions.

Then she shrugged away these odd thoughts. Tonight she would try to make her first ices. Then she would need to create a very special centrepiece, something to show *him* she was an artist as well as a tradeswoman.

She had not even thanked him for the machinery he had sent! Henrietta rushed to find pen and paper.

As she composed the stiff, formal phrases of thanks, her mind drifted off, wondering what the earl's entertainment would be like. What a pity she could not go herself. But Esau would deliver the centrepiece in the new handcart she had recently bought, with BASCOMBE'S in curly gold letters on the side.

Then she remembered one of the customers

telling her that Gunter's confectioner often went himself and put the finishing touches to the centrepiece just before it was carried to the table. But that would get her only as far as the kitchen.

Would he have a hostess? Henrietta drifted off into a rosy dream where she was standing by the earl's side, receiving his guests. She finally gave herself a little shake, signed the letter, sanded it, and sealed it. Her only interest in the earl, she told herself firmly, was to keep him amused and attracted enough to keep Bascombe's fashionable. Still...if she took the centrepiece along herself, she might be able to catch a glimpse of the ladies and see what they were like and what they were wearing. How could she know what kind of lady the earl found attractive if she never saw him with any?

CHAPTER SIX

A further formal note from the Earl of Carris-downe requested that Miss Bascombe bring the centrepiece to his house at seven on Friday evening so that it might be displayed to advantage in the refreshment room.

Henrietta toiled through the long nights before that Friday creating her masterpiece. The subject was the famous 'Battle of Salamanca,' which had taken place the previous July. It was the battle that did for Wellington what none of his previous battles had achieved. The world realised he had become 'almost a Marlborough'—to use the expression of General Foy, the only French commander to survive the battle with his corps intact.

As Josephine, Charlotte, Miss Hissop, and Esau watched, fascinated, the university city of Salamanca rose under Henrietta's inspired fingers. She had read long descriptions of the battle in the newspapers. There were the three forts, built out of the ruins of twenty colleges and thirteen convents, which had been garrisoned by Marmount when he retired from Salamanca at Wellington's approach, all made out of spun sugar and covered with caramel. There, created in miniature, was the River Torres with its green mats of waterweed, its sandbanks, and ancient water mills. A tiny, beautifully sculptured figure of Wellington on his horse stood in the plaza mayor while dainty Spanish ladies held out bouquets of flowers to him.

The Spanish ladies were all dressed in the fashion of Regency England because although the accounts that Henrietta had read of the battle were very extensive, none were detailed enough to sidetrack into a dissertation on the gowns worn by the ladies of Salamanca. Still, the confectionery figures wore mantillas of spun sugar and had black eyes made of tiny pieces of currant, so that their high-waisted gowns did not make them look so terriby un-Spanish.

Esau became worried again. He was jealous of the love and concentration Henrietta was lavishing on the centrepiece. Surely love for the earl, and only love, could inspire her thus. Esau had nightmares of Henrietta leaving on the arm of the Earl of Carrisdowne and not even throwing him one backward glance.

By Friday, Henrietta was finished and knew she had achieved something so great that she could never hope to repeat it.

The snow had melted and a soft wind, harbinger of spring, was blowing through the drying London streets. Blackbirds were carolling on the sooty roofs, and the sky above the twisted chimneys was a delicate violet as Henrietta and Esau set out with Henrietta's 'miracle' packed in layers of tissue paper on the handcart.

Henrietta had chosen to wear one of Josephine's warmer gowns. It was of gold velvet, high-waisted and buttoned with little velvet-covered buttons up to a small lace ruff at the neck. Over it she wore a heavy blue-wool cloak of her own.

When they reached the earl's house on Upper Brook Street, Henrietta felt her mouth grow dry with nerves.

Obviously she and Esau should manoeuvre the centrepiece down the area steps, which led under the main entrance to the kitchens below. But she persuaded herself that so much artistry should at least be rewarded by seeing the earl's reaction to it.

She left Esau on the pavement with the hand-cart and boldly mounted the front steps and sounded a brisk tattoo on the knocker.

The butler opened the door, looked at Henrietta, hatless and wrapped in a cloak that had seen better days, and demanded frostily, 'Yes?'

'I am come at Lord Carrisdowne's request,' said Henrietta grandly. She presented a visiting card turned down at the corner to show that she had called in person. 'Be so good as to take this card to his lordship.'

Impressed by her manner, the butler bowed and took the card. Then he saw Esau squinting up at him from the pavement. 'You boy,' said the butler. 'Be off with you, and don't stand there gawking.'

96

'That is my servant,' said Henrietta. 'Be so good as to take my card *immediately* to his lordship.'

The butler's face cleared. 'You're Bascombe's,' he said, looking at the curly lettering on the side of the cart. 'That must be the centrepiece. Wait there, and I'll send a footman to help you down to the kitchens with it.'

But, having come so far, Henrietta was not going to back down. 'I think,' she said sweetly, 'you will find his lordship expects to see me *in person.*' The butler hesitated. 'And,' went on Henrietta, 'I am sure he will be most annoyed if you keep me waiting out in the street much longer.'

'Very well,' said the butler reluctantly. He stood back and held open the door.

Henrietta blushed as she realized she would first have to help Esau lift the handcart up the shallow steps.

'I don't know as I should be allowing you to bring that in the front door,' muttered the butler as they trundled the cart past him. He turned and went up the stairs, leaving Henrietta and Esau standing in the hall.

Esau looked about him in awe. Apart from the cheerful crackling of logs in the hall fire, the town house was very hushed and quiet. The black and white tiles of the floor gleamed like glass. A chandelier of Waterford crystal sent prisms of coloured light over the pictures and wood panelling. A clock in the corner suddenly began to boom out seven o'clock and Esau jumped.

And then they heard the earl's voice. 'It is all right, Yarwood,' he said. 'Miss Bascombe is a friend of mine.'

The earl came slowly down the stairs, followed by his butler. He was already dressed for the evening in a black coat, black knee breeches, and shoes with diamond buckles. A large diamond flashed among the snowy folds of his cravat, and diamond rings sparkled on his fingers. His black hair was brushed and pomaded until it shone like a raven's wing.

Esau executed a clumsy bow from the waist, and Henrietta sank into a deep curtsy.

'Good evening, Miss Bascombe,' said the earl. 'The dining room, that is the door on your left—is to be used as a supper room this evening. If your servant will bring the centrepiece in there, we can arrange it to advantage.'

His manner was courteous and formal. Henrietta felt she had made a terrible mistake by entering by the front door. He led the way, and she turned to help Esau lift the centrepiece in its wrapping from the cart.

'My footmen will do that,' he said sharply.

But Henrietta shook her head. 'It is too fragile. Esau and I are used to handling these delicate confects.'

He gave an infinitesimal shrug and held open the door of the dining room. There was a long table against the wall, laden with plates, glasses, and knives and forks. Other long tables, spread with white-linen cloths, were set about the rest of the room.

'The food will be here,' said the earl, pointing to the table against the wall. 'My guests will fill their plates and then find a place at one of the other tables. The centrepiece goes on that raised platform in the middle of the table. I hope it is large enough?'

'Yes,' said Henrietta. Her heart was beating hard as she and Esau unwrapped the centrepiece and then lifted it gently onto the platform.

The earl was putting a log in the fire when Henrietta said, 'Do but look, my lord. I hope you are pleased with it.'

The earl turned and walked slowly back to where Henrietta was standing. He looked at the centrepiece, at the little figures, at the forts and the green river of angelica, at the Spanish ladies, and then at Wellington on his horse.

He looked at it a long time without saying a word. Henrietta felt tears start to her eyes.

He did not like it! And oh, how very tired she was.

'It is a masterpiece,' said the earl at last.

'You *like* it?' Henrietta blinked away her tears.

He raised her hand to his lips and kissed it.

'I was there,' he said, 'at Salamanca. You might have been there yourself, your work is so very good. It is amazing to think all this art is merely sugar to be eaten. How can I bear to let my guests even touch it? Miss Bascombe, please be my guest this evening. An artist such as yourself must see my friends' faces when they look on your work.'

'I should like that above all things,' exclaimed Henrietta. Then her face fell. 'But will it not be considered very odd to entertain your confectioner?'

He smiled. 'I think genius transcends social laws.'

'Perhaps if I am not *of* the party but merely sit in a corner and *observe*,' said Henrietta seriously, 'it would not be considered very odd.'

'As you will. My guests will sit down to supper at midnight. Come before then if you wish.'

'Midnight will do very well.'

'Good-bye, Miss Bascombe,' said the earl formally, his face once more unreadable.

After Henrietta and Esau had left, the Earl of Carrisdowne stood looking thoughtfully at the centrepiece. I cannot put her out of business, he thought. Such artistry must surely come before any plans to prevent a mistake by Charles or Guy. I am sure their intentions are not serious. They appear content to carry on mild flirtations. Perhaps I should mind my own business for a change.

Like Cinderella in reverse, Henrietta sat demurely in a corner of the Earl of Carrisdowne's dining room. When the clock struck twelve, her moment of glory would come.

She had been instructed by Josephine and Charlotte to observe Lord Charles and Mr Clifford and see which ladies they conversed with, and if either of them favoured any one in particular.

Henrietta was wearing a pink-satin slip with a Grecian frock of white Persian gauze, fastened up the front with silver filigree. The bottom was trimmed with a deep flounce of Vandyke lace. Everything she had on had been culled from all their wardrobes at the confectioner's. The gown was Josephine's, and the pearls around her neck belonged to Charlotte. They were Charlotte's most prized possession and the very last valuable thing she owned, all the rest having been sold. The silk flowers in Henrietta's glossy hair had been saved by Miss Hissop for twenty years and, unlike most of that poor lady's belongings, were as good as new, Miss Hissop having had to wear caps, since her twenty-third birthday as befitted her spinster state.

The earl had ordered his servants to carry the food in *after* the guests were all in the dining room. He did not want anything to detract from the centrepiece.

The clock struck twelve.

Two liveried footmen opened the double doors.

The Earl of Carrisdowne entered with a beautiful lady on his arm. Behind him came the rest of his guests. They clustered around the centrepiece, exclaiming in wonder and admiration.

But Henrietta heard none of it. There was a queer little ache in her heart as she watched the earl's handsome head next to the calm oval face of the beautiful woman. Who was she?

Not, thought Henrietta firmly, that I have a *tendre* for Carrisdowne or anything stupid like that. It is just...it is just that it would be wonderful to *belong* somewhere, instead of being a sort of strange social animal on the fringes of society.

Servants began carrying in dishes of meat, fruit, sweetmeats, and jellies. Henrietta's stomach gave a miserable rumble. She had been too excited to eat anything before leaving the shop.

Mr Clifford and Lord Charles were surrounded by a bevy of delightful-looking debutantes. 'And how can I tell either Josephine or Charlotte *that*?' worried Henrietta.

Henrietta sat as still as a statue in a dark corner of the room, partly hidden by a lacquered screen. The earl appeared to have forgotten her presence.

Henrietta would have been amazed had she known that he was aware of her presence during every minute of that supper.

Time dragged on. Henrietta wished she had not come.

Then finally the earl rose to his feet and proposed a toast to the King, the Prince Regent, and to the Duke of Wellington. He signalled to a servant to fill his glass again and said, 'My final toast of the evening is to the genius of Miss Bascombe, who created the centrepiece. Ladies and gentlemen, I give you...Miss Henrietta Bascombe.'

'Miss Henrietta Bascombe,' they all murmured.

Lord Charles, following his brother's gaze, cried, 'Why, there she is, over in that corner!'

Henrietta blushed with embarrassment and hung her head as every curious eye in the room turned in her direction.

The beautiful lady seated next to the earl broke the silence that followed Lord Charles's announcement.

'Well, it *is* for *eating*, isn't it?' she demanded.

'Lady Clara, it is much too beautiful to touch,' protested Mr Clifford.

'Nonsense,' said Lady Clara. She rose gracefully to her feet and walked over to the centrepiece. 'See!' she cried, picking up the Duke of Wellington. 'I shall let you all know if our Iron Duke tastes of iron or sugar.' She bit off the little figure's head.

Almost everyone laughed, got to his or her feet and started snatching at pieces off the confection.

Lady Clara *who?* thought Henrietta. Miss Hissop will know.

Henrietta, sensing that the people in the room had forgotten her existence once more, felt more at ease than she had earlier. She carefully observed Lord Charles and Mr Clifford. They did not seem at all interested in any of the ladies present. *They* had not rushed to help destroy the centrepiece, nor had the earl.

Of course, this was not really seeing society at its best, thought Henrietta charitably. A great number of them, the ladies as well as the gentlemen, were in varying stages of intoxication. And why should she, Henrietta Bascombe, take such a fierce dislike to that Lady Clara?

My centrepieces *are* for *eating*, Henrietta told herself firmly.

The earl rose to his feet once more and announced that dancing would begin in the ballroom upstairs. The guests began to leave the dining room, first in large groups, then one by one, until Henrietta was left alone, except for the servants, who were clearing away the plates.

She got to her feet and walked across the room and looked down at the ruin of her centrepiece. One tiny little Spanish lady stood amid the wreck of sugar, marzipan, and caramel, her tiny bouquet held up to where the figure of the duke had been.

'I do not know how they could bear to eat even a bit of it,' said a voice behind her. 'It was so beautiful.' Henrietta turned around and found Mr Clifford had come back into the room.

'Usually I do not witness their destruction Mr Clifford,' she said. 'But imagine if people could not bear to eat any of my confects. I should soon go out of business.'

'How is Miss Archer...and Mrs Webster?' asked Mr Clifford.

'Very well. They are asleep by now. Poor things! They are beginning to feel the strain of all those weeks of hard work.'

Mr Clifford glanced over his shoulder nervously. 'Miss Bascombe,' he said, 'since Bascombe's *is* your business, I feel you are responsible for Miss Archer. May I have your permission to call on her?'

'Yes,' smiled Henrietta.

'And, oh, I say...' Again that nervous look over the shoulder. 'Charles—I mean, Lord Charles—well, he begged me to ask you on his behalf. If he could call on Mrs Webster, that is.'

'Perhaps Lord Carrisdowne would not approve,' said Henrietta cautiously.

'If he didn't know about it, he wouldn't have to worry about it,' said Mr Clifford.

The earl's voice, giving orders to the servants, came from the hall outside.

'*Please*, Miss Bascombe,' said Mr Clifford urgently.

How ridiculous to be so afraid of one's best friend, thought Henrietta. Aloud she said, 'You and Lord Charles may come for dinner next Sunday—at four.'

The Earl of Carrisdowne walked into the room.

Mr Clifford pleaded with his eyes for Henrietta's silence, and Henrietta gave him a slight nod to signify assent.

The earl looked from one to the other suspiciously.

'I am just leaving,' said Mr Clifford hurriedly. 'Your servant, Miss Bascombe.' He bowed and left. The earl swivelled and looked after him.

'Dear me, one would think Guy was making an assignation.'

'With me? No. We were just admiring the last survivor.' Henrietta held up the sugar figure of the Spanish lady.

'Yes.' He took it from her and turned it around in the light. 'I must confess my heart sank when they started tearing into it like wolves. Perhaps I was too conscious of your clear gaze looking upon my friends, for I confess they seemed a shabby lot to me this evening.'

'I know most of them by sight,' said Henrietta. 'They are my customers. They are all very pleasant and quite witty. I had not, however, seen Lady Clara before.'

'But you know of her?'

'No. I heard her name mentioned.'

'She is Lady Clara Sinclair, daughter of the Earl of Strathbane.'

'Oh.'

'She is this season's beauty.'

'Ah.'

'She is accounted a wit.'

'Mm.'

'As you so cynically remark, "Mm" indeed. Lady Clara told me a very funny story at supper that went on for quite half an hour. It was about Lord Trumpington, who was asked to lay a foundation stone at a new printing works in Kensington. He was given a silver trowel to perform the ceremony. He expected to keep the trowel as a present but, to his fury, the printers demanded it back. He was, says Clara, very *mortar-fied.*'

Henrietta laughed dutifully.

'Don't force yourself,' he drawled. 'I cannot stand puns either. My face is stiff with forcing smiles onto it. Can I persuade you to come and watch the dancing?'

A shadow crossed Henrietta's face. Of course he could not ask her to dance with him.

'No, thank you, my lord,' she said. 'It is time I returned to my shop. The baking for tomorrow has still to be done.'

He looked down at her, noticing for the first time the violet shadows of fatigue under her eyes. 'I would you did not have to work so hard,' he said. 'Come driving with me on Sunday, Miss Bascombe.'

'I cannot,' said Henrietta, with a faint blush. 'I am entertaining guests for dinner.'

He looked at her sharply.

'*Female* guests?'

'I must go,' said Henrietta, not answering his question.

'Where is your servant?'

'In bed.'

'You cannot walk unescorted through the streets in the middle of the night. I shall send a footman with you. No, I shall go with you myself.'

'My lord...your guests.'

'So busy polishing their puns, they will not miss me.'

Henrietta enjoyed a novel sensation of power. It was very pleasant to think she could make the earl leave his guests.

To her surprise the earl, as he had done when he escorted her to church, elected to walk. This was decidedly odd behaviour in an age when one travelled by carriage even to the next street.

'Tell me about yourselves,' said the earl. 'Where did all of you come from?'

Henrietta hesitated. For the sake of Josephine's safety, she did not wish to mention the name of the village. She still did not trust the earl.

'We all come from the same village in the country,' she said. 'My father was a doctor who died leaving me hardly any money. Miss Hissop is a retired schoolmistress. We decided to pool our small savings and share a house. A certain landowner who had been attended by my father during his lifetime and had never paid his bills left me a sum of money in his will. I decided to go into trade. The landowner's chef had trained me in the confectioner's art. Mrs Webster is an army widow with practically no money at all. She is only twenty-two years of age. Miss Archer has a brutal father who beat her every time he was drunk. They elected to join me in my enterprise.'

'And what draws Mr Clifford and Lord Charles to your shop? Yourself?'

'I think gentlemen of the ton enjoy the sweetmeats and the comfortable atmosphere,' said Henrietta.

'That is not answering my question. What was Guy talking to you about?'

'He was regretting the destruction of my centrepiece.'

'And that was all?'

'Lord Carrisdowne, you must not quiz me about who said what to me. I am too tired.'

'Do not encourage them,' he said in a serious voice. 'Marriage is out of the question.'

Henrietta rounded on him. 'May I suggest you run your *own* life and stop meddling in affairs that do not concern you!'

Henrietta was shaken by fury and bitterness. He had more or less told her she was not worth considering when it came to marriage. He had told her as much before but, oh *how* it hurt this time. Her eyes filled with tears, and the parish lamps became a flickering blur.

He stopped and swung her round to face him. He took out a handkerchief and gently dried her eyes. 'Ah, no, Henrietta,' he said softly, 'you must not cry. It was your evening of triumph.' He bent and kissed her cheek.

Henrietta trembled, looking at him wide-eyed.

He wanted to pull her into his arms and kiss her breathless. He wanted to do just that with an intensity of feeling that shook him. Instead he tucked her hand under his arm and started to walk again.

'How did you know my Christian name?' asked Henrietta.

'I asked someone. It is not a deathly secret, you know. The other ladies in the shop call you Henrietta frequently.'

They had reached the shop.

Henrietta turned and faced him. His diamonds glinted in the faint light thrown by the parish lamp outside the door of Bascombe's. But his face was in shadow and she could not read the expression in his eyes.

'I did not like to see you sitting in that corner while I entertained much less talented people,' he said. 'Allow me to entertain you to dinner tomorrow night.'

'I cannot go to your house alone,' said Henrietta backing away.

'Then bring your dragon, what is her name... Miss Hissop.'

Henrietta was about to refuse. But it was so very tempting—tempting only because it would be wonderful to be waited on for a change.

'Yes, my lord,' she said. 'At what time?'

'Seven o'clock. I shall send the carriage for you?'

He raised her hand to his lips, and his kiss seemed to burn through her glove. Then he stood back and waited until she had unlocked the shop door before walking away.

I only think I am enchanted with her because I see so little of her, thought the earl. Tomorrow evening she will be out of place and gauche, a country girl out of her depth. That should cure these odd feelings she arouses in me.

Henrietta neary fell over Esau, who was sleeping like a dog on the floor of the shop behind the door. 'I waited for you, miss,' said Esau, jumping to his feet. 'I got something to show you.'

He led the way into the kitchen. There on the table was a sugar dragon on a sugar horse. The horse was excellent. The figure on its back was somewhat lumpy.

'It is very good, Esau,' said Henrietta. 'Very good indeed.'

She leaned forward, studying the figure closely while her mind worked busily. Here was surely Esau's future. If she could manage to get Josephine and Charlotte settled comfortably, then Esau could be trained to take over the business.

'You need some lessons, all the same,' said Henrietta slowly. 'As soon as the business settles down, I shall begin to train you to be a confectioner.'

'Oh, thank you, miss. You should ha' let me come to fetch you. Don't do to walk the streets alone.'

'I was not alone,' said Henrietta vaguely, her mind full of plans. 'Lord Carrisdowne escorted me.'

'Oh,' said Esau, turning away. 'He did, did he?'

CHAPTER SEVEN

Henrietta's casual remark that she and Miss Hissop were invited to the Earl of Carrisdowne's for dinner that evening burst upon the confectioner's shop like a bombshell the next morning. And when Henrietta added that Lord Charles Worsley and Mr Guy Clifford were to be their guests at dinner the coming Sunday, excitement reached fever pitch.

Respectability at last! Josephine and Charlotte dreamed of a triple wedding—Josephine to Mr Clifford, Charlotte to Lord Charles, and Henrietta to the Earl of Carrisdowne.

Miss Hissop was incoherent with excitement. 'To think that I...Ismene Hissop...should dine at a lord's table! He means *well*...wouldn't have invited *me* otherwise. Dear Henrietta...who knows what social peaks we may scale! Why, one could even be buried in Westminster Abbey!'

The only one depressed by the great news was Esau. His active conscience told him he should wish the best for his mistress, but it was shouted down by his terror at having to return to the workhouse.

Henrietta made such an effort with her appearance that evening that Esau felt she was removing herself even more from the shop, from him. Henrietta in her apron and cap was a world apart from the grand lady who now stood at the shop door with Miss Hissop, waiting for the earl's carriage. Josephine had said that she hoped Henrietta would order some gowns for herself, for now that she had hopes of being taken out by Mr Clifford, she would need all her own gowns.

Henrietta was wearing a dress of white leno, trimmed with a narrow edging of lace. A scarf of pink Italian gauze was tied on the left shoulder with gold cord, the gold tassels hanging nearly to the feet. She had little white kid shoes with gold roses on her feet and long gloves of white kid. Her dark brown hair was braided into a little coronet on top of her head and decorated with a single pink-silk rose.

Miss Hissop had dipped into Josephine's wardrobe herself and had chosen a brown-silk gown and a handsome paisley shawl. Charlotte's pearls were about her neck, and one of her more elaborate caps, freshly laundered and starched, covered her head.

'There is the carriage,' said Henrietta, feeling quite sick with excitement. She kissed Josephine and Charlotte and then followed Miss Hissop out of the shop.

Miss Hissop exclaimed over the elegance of the carriage, at the wine-coloured upholstery, at the hot bricks that had been placed on the floor for their feet. The journey was all too short—along Half Moon Street, up Curzon Street, along South Audley Street, past Grosvenor Square, and round into Upper Brook Street.

Henrietta hoped they would not be the only guests. If the earl presented her to some of his friends and showed them she was a welcome guest in his house, Henrietta felt it would set the seal on her respectability. But, as they were ushered into the Green Saloon, it soon transpired they were, in fact, the only guests. It was this fact that made Henrietta silent and awkward.

The earl put her uneasiness down to the fact that she was overawed by her surroundings. It was just as he had expected.

But over dinner Henrietta became a different lady entirely. To put her at her ease, for he was feeling sorry for her, the earl politely asked her about her late father's profession.

Henrietta, at first hesitantly and then with enthusiasm, described her father's work. 'He was wont to say,' said Henrietta, 'that a fifth-century Greek had probably had a better chance of recovery under Hippocrates than the people of today. How he had battled with prejudice and superstition and antiquated ideas! He had vaccinated the whole village against the smallpox, and mostly at his own expense. He had also written letters to Parliament and to the newspapers complaining about the window tax. By bricking up his windows, a householder could save a great deal on tax, but in doing so he shut out the sun and fresh air. Then the villagers *would* dose their children with Dr James's Powder, and it is a wonder so many survived. My father analyzed the powder and found it contained antimony.' Her soft voice went on, and her eyes glowed with enthusiasm.

She should have been a man, thought the earl. Why could she not have waited until she was married before indulging her odd tastes for independence. Married ladies were allowed great licence. Not that such licence included going into trade, he reminded himself firmly.

He realized with a start that Henrietta was not at all overawed by her surroundings. On the contrary, she seemed very much part of them.

Miss Hissop, seeing his startled look, decided he was shocked that Henrietta should discourse at length on medicine, a subject that should only be debated by gentlemen. She gave a little cough, and when Henrietta stopped talking and turned an inquiring gaze on her, Miss Hissop launched into speech. 'Your admiration of your dear papa does you credit, Henrietta. But to hear you speak, one would think your pretty head was full of naught but serious matters. My lord could not guess how many happy hours we have spent discussing the latest romance from the circulating library, or how we avidly study the latest fashion.'

'My dear Miss Hissop,' said Henrietta, 'we were so busy keeping body and soul together when we were in...in the country, that we had no time to talk about such things. All we ever talked about then was food. All we ever talk about now is the shop. Since my lord disapproves of trade, he must be grateful that I confine my conversation to medicine.'

'I like hearing about the shop,' protested the earl, much to his own surprise. 'Have you made ices yet?'

'Yes, at last. The first few tries were unsuccessful. I hate to waste materials. My one main problem at the moment is how to get people to *pay* for their centrepieces.'

'Henrietta!' exclaimed Miss Hissop.

'But it is the truth. Here is a society that does

118

not believe in paying shopkeepers, tailors, or jewellers until the duns come to the door. How can I make them pay?'

'It is a difficult question,' he agreed, reflecting that he had not yet paid Henrietta's modest bill himself either.

'Now dressmakers do not have quite the same problem since they call on the lady of the house. Provided their fashions are in demand, the lady in question becomes afraid that if she does not pay, then she will lose her favourite dressmaker,' the earl continued.

'Now you, Miss Bascombe, could request the money *in advance*. Say firmly that you wish to buy the best of materials and cannot do that without money in hand. At the moment, it is fashionable to have one of your centrepieces rather than one of Gunter's. Society will always pay to be the fashion. It is rumoured that Mr Brummell once paid his tailor.'

'What a good idea!' cried Henrietta. 'It will make me appear very mercenary and pushing, but I cannot let niceties get in the way of making a profit.'

'Does money mean so much to you?' he asked curiously.

'All the world!' laughed Henrietta. 'It means all the world to me. It can buy warmth and comfort and food, all those things of which I have been too long deprived. I would do anything for money!'

'Anything?' he mocked.

'In the way of business,' said Henrietta severely.

They eventually retired to the saloon, the earl electing to join them rather than be left to his wine in solitary splendour.

Miss Hissop, overcome by too much food and wine, fell asleep in a chair by the fire. Henrietta sitting beside the earl on a sofa, coughed loudly several times, hoping to wake up her chaperon. But Miss Hissop began to snore gently.

'Leave her,' said the earl in an amused voice. 'You are safe with me...I think.'

He took both her hands in his and looked down into her eyes. He had thought it would be easy to make her fall in love with him. He had not realized until now how easy it would be for *him* to fall in love with *her*.

She tried to pull her hands away, but he held on to them tightly. Her soft mouth trembled, and her eyelashes were fanned out over her cheeks.

He gave an impatient little exclamation and pulled her into his arms. She made a muffled protest as his mouth came down on hers. It was meant to be a light, teasing kiss, but no sooner did the earl taste the warmth of her mouth and feel her bosom pressing against his chest than he lost his senses and kissed her with all the passion he had never known he could hold for any woman.

He was brought to his senses by Henrietta's little hands beating frantically against his shoulders.

'Forgive me,' he said huskily.

'No,' said Henrietta crossly, moving away from him. 'You would not have behaved *thus* with a lady.'

'I have never been so bewitched in my life before,' he said. 'Oh, Henrietta, come driving with me on Sunday—alone.'

'My dinner party.'

'To the deuce with it. Who are these people who are so important?'

Henrietta longed to tell him, but he might grow hard and angry again—and he might try to ruin her business.

'No one of importance,' she said, hanging her head.

Miss Hissop awoke with a start. Henrietta rose to her feet, saying she must leave, the hour was late, and she had work to do.

The earl longed for another moment with Henrietta so that he might try to find out the names of her dinner party guests. Why had she not invited *him*, damn it, he thought furiously, forgetting that only a short time ago he would have considered Miss Bascombe to be addled in her wits if she had issued such an invitation.

Henrietta was silent on the road home, wrestling with uncomfortable thoughts. She had wanted the earl to go on kissing her, and surely no lady entertained ideas such as that.

But her eyes were soft, and her face was glowing as she stepped into the shop. Sadly Esau watched her. Unless he thought of something, and quickly, then Henrietta would be leaving him to get married.

The earl met his friend, Guy Clifford, in Gentleman Jackson's Boxing Saloon on Saturday afternoon. 'There's a prizefight in Cobham on Sunday,' said the earl. 'Care to come along?'

'I can't,' said Mr Clifford, turning away. 'Have a most important engagement.'

'Where?'

'I don't need to tell you everything,' said Mr Clifford. 'You ain't my father.'

The earl let the subject drop, although his mind began to race.

He stayed for a bout with the famous Jackson and then strolled homeward. His younger brother was just leaving as he arrived at Upper

Brook Street. 'Off to Bascombe's again?' asked the earl sweetly.

'Go there too much,' said Lord Charles airily. 'Get a bit tired of seeing nothing but females. Taking myself off to the club for a rubber.'

'Learning sense in your old age,' grinned the earl. 'There's a prizefight at Cobham tomorrow. Care to accompany me?'

'No, no,' said Lord Charles hurriedly. 'Doing something else. Forget what. But definitely something else.'

He hurried down the street and left the earl looking suspiciously after him. 'Now,' thought the Earl of Carrisdowne, stroking his chin. 'I wonder. I just wonder...'

Henrietta's dinner party was a delightfully informal affair. It was served at the country hour of four in the afternoon. Charlotte and Josephine were looking their prettiest.

Lord Charles was amazed when Miss Hissop told him that she and Henrietta had been to Upper Brook Street for dinner. 'What a sly fox Rupert is,' said Lord Charles. 'I was away that evening at a play and then a rout. He said nothing to me.'

'Well, seems he can't say anything about *us* socializing,' said Mr Clifford cheerfully.

Both gentlemen suggested they take Josephine and Charlotte out driving. Henrietta was closing the shop during the last week in Lent to get in extra supplies for the Season. Mr Clifford proposed they should all go for a picnic if the weather should prove fine, 'and no doubt Rupert will want to go with us.'

'I should not say anything...just yet,' advised Henrietta.

'But he can't ask *you* to dinner and then forbid *us* to take out Mrs Webster and Miss Archer,' protested Lord Charles.

'He just might,' said Henrietta. 'Which is why I did not tell him you were both coming here today. Oh, do not look so downcast! Let us not talk about the Earl of Carrisdowne.'

The dinner proceeded merrily until at last Lord Charles and Mr Clifford rose to take their leave. Henrietta waved to them from the step.

From the corner of Half Moon Street, Jean, the earl's devoted Swiss valet, watched them go. Some ten minutes later he was standing before his master in the earl's study.

'Yes?' said the earl curtly. He was feeling rather grubby. It had seemed a good idea when he had sent Jean to spy on Bascombe's. Now he was so sure Henrietta's dinner guests would turn out to be a mere gaggle of females and leave him with all the guilt of having been suspicious of her.

The Swiss looked at the cornice. 'Lord Charles and Mr Clifford were the guests,' he said. 'Miss Bascombe herself waved good-bye to them. They appeared to be on the best of terms.'

'Thank you,' said the earl quietly. 'You may go. I need not remind you, I trust, to be discreet?'

'I am always discreet,' said Jean, adding with the licence of an old and trusted servant, 'as you have reason to know.'

When he had left, the earl sat glaring at the wall opposite, consumed with rage. Henrietta Bascombe was not an innocent. She was devious and scheming. The very fact that she had not told him the names of her guests showed that she wished to entrap one of them for herself. When she might have had *you*, jeered a little voice in his head. 'I was never, at any time, in danger of allying my great name with that of a shopgirl,' he told the uncaring serried ranks of books above his desk.

He tried to force himself into a calmer frame of mind. To rail at Guy and Charles might give Henrietta the added lustre of forbidden fruit. What was she playing at? I shall ask her, he thought.

And so Henrietta, who was helping the

others to wash and put away the dinner dishes, was startled at the sound of loud knocking at the door.

Religious Esau had gone to evening service.

She went to the shop door, raised the blind, and looked through the glass—and reeled backward before the angry glare of the Earl of Carrisdowne, who was standing on the step outside.

She knew, instinctively, that somehow he had found out about the visit of Lord Charles and Mr Clifford.

She signalled to him to wait, and without telling the others anything, ran upstairs to fetch her bonnet and cloak. Anything the Earl of Carrisdowne had to say to her, he could say out of the hearing of the others. Josephine and Charlotte must not have their splendid day spoiled.

The earl was just raising his hand to knock again when he saw Henrietta on the other side of the glass, unlocking the door.

She put a finger to her lips as he would have burst into angry speech there and then. 'Walk with me a little, my lord,' said Henrietta. 'I do not wish to upset the others with an angry scene.'

'And just how do you know it is going to be an angry scene, Miss Shopkeeper?'

'Because you are breathing fire and brimstone,' said Henrietta calmly. 'Hold your fire until we get to the Green Park.'

'I do not think I want to walk about a damp park in the darkness,' he said.

'You have no choice, my lord,' replied Henrietta, 'for I am not going to have a verbal boxing match with you in the street..'

They entered the park and walked a little way under the trees. Finally she stopped and turned to face him. 'I surmise you have discovered my guests today were Lord Charles Worsley and Mr Clifford.'

'Yes.'

'And why should that make you so very angry?'

'I *warned* you, madam, that I would do my utmost to protect my brother and friend from making unsuitable alliances.'

'Then, perhaps you should set a better example. Inviting me to dinner encouraged both to believe they might have your approval.'

'Don't play Miss Innocent with me,' he said, his voice low and intense. 'You refused to name your guests. *That* shows a guilty conscience.'

'You did not tell either Lord Charles or Mr Clifford that *I* had been *your* guest.'

'That is different.'

'I see no difference.'

'You are mocking me,' he raged, 'because you have managed to enslave my friend and my brother.'

'No!' exclaimed Henrietta, too surprised to do other than tell the truth. 'Mr Clifford favours Miss Archer and Lord Charles, Mrs Webster. Now Charlotte, Mrs Webster, has been married before, but that is all to the good. She has a certain wisdom and maturity beyond her years that balances Lord Charles's lack of both..'

'How dare you criticize my brother!'

Henrietta spoke in a weary little voice. 'It is of no use. You are determined to find us all socially unacceptable. But think, might Lord Charles not be better with a lady of gentle birth who works in a shop than some debutante who will marry him for his money and title and then will probably be unfaithful to him after marriage, like so many of the married women in society. And Miss Archer—Josephine—what is there so monstrous about *her* to merit your censure? She is not bold, nor vulgar. But all this is a mere waste of time. I will not apologize to you for inviting Mr Clifford and Lord Charles, neither will I apologize for not telling you that they were my guests. You are every bit as angry and unreasonable as I expected you to be.'

'I...am...never...unreasonable,' he grated.

'Then, you might appreciate the reason in this. Since it is obvious you will never leave us in peace. I shall tell Josephine and Charlotte that they must never see either your brother or Mr Clifford again.

'You, my reasonable lord, must also understand that I never want to see *you* again. Just leave my business alone.' Her voice broke on a sob as she added, 'I am so very tired, you know, and...and...there is so much work to be done. I have neither the time nor the energy to cross words with you.'

She turned and began to walk slowly away from him across the grass, a dim figure under the trees.

'Wait!' he cried. 'Please wait, Miss Bascombe.'

One thing she had said burst upon his brain like a skyrocket. Neither Charles nor Guy were interested in *her*. She had merely been trying to do the best for her friends.

He must not lose her.

'What is it now?' demanded Henrietta in a tired little voice.

The great attraction she held for him battled with his pride. Attraction won.

'Forgive me,' he said. 'I have been autocratic ...bullying...hasty. There has been much care and responsibility put on me since the death of my father. I spoke rashly. I shall not stand in the way of either Charles or Guy. There! Please smile and say you will let me take you driving. Or to the theatre.'

Henrietta's spirits rose from the depths to the heavens in one bound. She could not stay angry with him. Was he smiling? She wished it were not so dark so that she might see his face.

'I should like that very much,' she said, and the bewitched earl felt he had never before heard such beautiful words in his life. 'Only wait until the shop is closed during the last week in Lent. *Then* I shall have some free time.

'In fact, Mr Clifford and Lord Charles plan to take Mrs Webster and Miss Archer on a picnic during that week. Perhaps we could go with them.'

'Of course.' He wanted to pull her into his arms, but something held him back. Not knowing that that *something* was the first little step toward marriage, the Earl of Carrisdowne drew Henrietta's arm through his and, in a companionable silence, they walked slowly together, back to the shop on Half Moon Street.

CHAPTER EIGHT

Before the great day of the picnic, Lord Charles Worsley met Mr Guy Clifford on New Bond Street. It was Lord Charles who had now become the intimate of Mr Clifford, the earl being immersed in various business ventures on the stock exchange. Gentlemen could gamble on the stock exchange. That was not sullied by the name of 'trade.' The two had been drawn together by their love for the ladies of the bakery.

They did not know of the earl's increasing fondness for Henrietta, only that, somehow, he had found out about that dinner party and had surprised them by appearing amused rather than angry. He had next amazed them by saying he planned to be present at the famous picnic. After much debate and decision, a journey to the Surrey fields was settled on.

'Where are you bound, Guy?' asked Lord Charles.

'I am going into labour,' said Mr Clifford.

Lord Charles pursed his lips in a soundless whistle. 'Going into labour' meant being fitted into a new pair of leather breeches. Mr Clifford must be very much in love to elect to go through such an agonizing performance.

'I'll come with you and be in at the birth,' said Lord Charles.

They turned in at the breeches maker—this personage was never called a tailor; breeches makers working in leather were considered of a higher order.

Mr Clifford groaned in anticipation as the new leather breeches of pale leather were produced.

The breeches maker summoned four sturdy assistants, and Mr Clifford lay on a blanket on the shop floor.

Lord Charles lent a hand and all pulled and tugged and strained to fit the skintight breeches up over Mr Clifford's thighs and bottom.

'Wriggle a bit,' said Lord Charles. 'Try a bit harder. We're nearly there.'

A final massive pull and the breeches were safely up around Mr Clifford's waist. A special instrument had to be produced to button them.

Then, stiff as a board, Mr Clifford was lifted and propped upright. He had to be supported while he kicked out with one leg and then the other to ease the stiffness of the leather.

'Very nice,' commented Lord Charles. 'Like the ladies' muslins, they leave little to the imagination. Now, we'll all need to take a deep breath and get 'em off again.'

'No,' said Mr Clifford, 'Leave 'em on, for pity's sake. I'll sleep in them if need be.'

'Yes, but you do have a tendency to creak,' protested Lord Charles as they strolled out of the shop—or rather Lord Charles strolled while Mr Clifford took painful mincing steps.

'What colour d'ye call that?' demanded Lord Charles, levelling his quizzing glass at the breeches. 'Mud of Paris,' said Mr Clifford. 'It was a choice between that or Emperor's Eye.'

'Horrible names they have for colours,' sighed Lord Charles. 'Slaves of fashion, that's what we are. Now take these pantaloons of mine. Don't like the colour. But my tailor tells me I must have pantaloons of a reddish colour. All on the reds, now, my lord,' he says, and so red it is. We are tyrannized by this street.' He waved his quizzing glass at New Bond Street. 'One week it's one thing and the next, t'other. Do you remember a couple of years back when all our boots had to have leather wrinkled on the insole and all *that* did was to retain the dirt and baffle the shoe-black. As for the ladies— twenty years ago they all had waists and hoops. Now that they've started casting off their clothes, they don't know where to stop. You're never wearing those torture chambers of breeches to the picnic?'

'Of course I am. They will have eased out by then.'

Perhaps if Mr Clifford had worn the breeches during the days before the picnic, they might have become more comfortable but, having got them off that night, he found himself very reluctant to put them on again.

But love gave him the courage to suffer and, when the great day dawned, bright and sunny, he was crammed back into them by his valet, his cook, and his knife boy.

They set out in procession from the bakery, the Earl of Carrisdowne driving Henrietta and Miss Hissop, Lord Charles in his carriage driving Charlotte and Josephine and Guy Clifford and, behind that, the earl's fourgon with his servants and enough food and drink to feed a detachment of dragoons.

Although the earl was supplying food and servants for the outing, Mr Clifford was the one who had chosen the spot for the picnic. To his dismay, when they arrived at the chosen spot, he found it occupied by a band of evil-looking Gypsies.

The earl, who was chatting to Henrietta and Miss Hissop about a play he had seen the previous week, was content to leave it to Mr

Clifford to find somewhere else.

Mr Clifford, thrown into a fever of anxiety and wanting only the best for Josephine, directed Lord Charles's carriage to lead the way, and then hung on to the guardrail, shouting from time to time, 'Stop! No...that will not do. Try farther on.'

At last the earl became aware that he was very hungry and that they had been travelling for quite a long time, and called sharply to Mr Clifford to find *somewhere*, or they would all find themselves in the Channel.

Josephine said timidly that she was feeling very hungry, too, and alarmed that he should cause his beloved the slightest distress, Mr Clifford picked the first lane that led to the nearest field and declared it was just the thing.

Stiffly they all climbed down from the carriages and looked about them. It was a square field bordered by a high thorn hedge, nothing more. No stream, no trees, no pretty prospect.

Above, the blue of the sky had changed to a milky colour, and a scudding, irritating little wind had got up, snatching at hats and bonnets.

The servants spread rugs and cushions on the grass and began to unload all the impedimenta of spirit stove, hampers, and bottles.

The wind grew stronger. The earl suggested that they move everything to the edge of the field so that they might gain some shelter from the hedge. But Mr Clifford, exhilarated with being in command for once, pooh-poohed the idea and said they were all to sharp-set to fuss.

Conversation grew desultory as bits of grass blew into glasses of wine, and the increasing chill of the wind cut through the muslins of the ladies.

'It will not do,' said Miss Hissop at last. 'I am aware the damp from the ground is seeping through this rug. I shall catch the ague. Woe is me! Oh, that I must be snatched from this earth before my moment of glory!'

'What moment of glory?' demanded the earl, eyeing the steadily darkening sky uneasily. They had travelled in open carriages and he was now worried they would be soaked before they could reach London again.

'Everlasting glory,' said Henrietta, throwing Miss Hissop a warning look. She knew that Miss Hissop dreamed of attending all three girls as bridesmaid.

The earl, who had now heard Miss Hissop talking about her plans for her own funeral several times, accepted Henrietta's explanation and assumed Miss Hissop was thinking of the hereafter, unaware that the spinster obviously expected her moment of glory to come in this world and not the next.

Henrietta was disappointed. She had looked forward to a sylvan setting where Charlotte and Josephine would stroll beside a little stream, talking to their beaux. She had never thought for a moment they would be attended by a retinue of servants. It made the whole business as formal as a dining room.

There were fortunately plenty of fur carriage rugs to supply cloaks for the ladies, but the wind was growing colder by the minute. With cold fingers, they nibbled at wafers of Westphalian ham and slices of chicken. No one felt like eating much in such uncomfortable circumstances.

At last the earl rose. 'Walk with me a little,' he said to Henrietta. 'I fear we must leave soon. I cannot blame Guy for his lack or organization. We were all mad to venture out on a picnic when the leaves are not yet on the trees. The poet Milton describes the souls of the condemned as being hurried from fiery into frozen regions. Perhaps his imagination was fired by such a day as this. I consider myself a sensible man, and yet, like most Englishmen, I am frequently surprised at the vagaries of the weather. We all all put ourselves at the mercy of this fickle climate. Why do we not warm our rooms like the Germans, with a closed stove and pipes to carry the heat around the walls? Because we say we like to see the fire. "It is so dismal not to see the fire," we say. And so, for the sake of seeing the fire, we are frozen on one side and roasted on the other. We have more women and children killed because of hearth deaths, *burned* to death, in one year than all the heretics and witches who were ever burned at the stake. We—'

'If you wish to continue your speech,' interrupted Henrietta with a shiver, 'pray let us go over by the hedge, where we may be sheltered from the wind.'

They walked over and stood by the tall thorn hedge. The wind moaned and hissed through its branches, making a desolate sound.

'There will be hot tea soon,' said the earl, looking along the line of trees to where his servants were crouched round the spirit stove, trying to shelter the flame from the wind.

'Poor things,' said Henrietta, meaning the servants. 'They must be very cold. At least *their* carriage is covered, and they are not in danger of freezing on the road back. Being a sort of servant oneself changes one's view of things very much.'

'I do not like to hear you talk thus.'

'But it is true,' said Henrietta, looking anxiously up into his face. 'I now belong to the serving class. There is a poem on the kitchen wall left by the previous tenants. It goes:

Next, as we're servants, Masters at our Hands
Expect obedience to all just Commands;
Which, if we rightly think is but their Due,
Nor more than we in Reason ought to do.
Purchas'd by annual Wages, Cloths, and Meat,
Theirs is our Time, our Hands, our Heads, our
    Feet:
We think, design, and act at their Command,
And, as their Pleasure varies, walk or stand;
Whilst we receive the convenanted Hire,
Active Obedience justly they require...

'I have forgotten the rest. But, you see, I cannot help noticing that your butler is quite blue with cold and that the serving maids do not have cloaks or pelisses to keep them warm.'

'I am not a monster,' said the earl impatiently. 'My servants are well housed and well fed. The reason they are not more warmly dressed is for the same reason *we* are not warmly dressed. They are English, too, and like all the English, they have only to see a sunny morn to be convinced the day will remain fine until sundown.

'Were my Swiss here, he would now be muffled to the eyeballs, having brought along suitable clothes for at least six changes of climate. But if it distresses you to see cold servants, then warm servants you shall have. I do not think we should freeze in this draughty field, waiting for tea. I shall send them all home, and I suggest we repair to the nearest inn and sit in front of a roaring fire and drink tea there.'

One large flake of snow spiralled down over the hedge and landed on Henrietta's nose. He took out his handkerchief and brushed it away. 'See what I mean?' he teased. 'We are about to find ourselves in a sort of arctic if we do not move.' He walked away to order the servants to go.

Henrietta happily saw that Josephine and Charlotte now appeared impervious to the cold as they chatted to Lord Charles and Mr Clifford. Charlotte looked a different girl from the pale beauty of the Charlotte of the village. Her cheeks were tinged with healthy pink, and her eyes sparkled. As Henrietta crossed the field to join them, the wind struck her with a roar, and the field all but disappeared in a roaring white blizzard.

The horses had been unharnessed from the carriages and allowed to graze. The earl called to Lord Charles and Mr Clifford to help him harness them up so that the servants might be free to pack everything away in the fourgon.

The ladies were bundled up in rugs in the carriages. Miss Hissop was gasping and wailing that the end was nigh, and Henrietta resisted a strong temptation to slap her. Yet Henrietta was so busy mouring the wreck of the day for Josephine and Charlotte, she had little time to examine her own feelings.

She persuaded herself that she was glad the earl showed no signs of wanting to kiss her again. She admitted she enjoyed his company, but that was a good thing, and a bonus in a way, since her only interest in him lay in keeping Bascombe's a fashionable establishment.

As they inched their way through the blinding, wet snow, the earl, on the other hand, was thinking a great deal about Henrietta, and had to admit to himself he was puzzled by her attitude.

Although she appeared pleased to be with him, there was a certain detachment about her. Remembering that kiss had meant so much to him, he decided reluctantly that it had meant very little to her. She did not appear at all embarrassed or flustered in his company.

Only that morning the earl had thought it folly to take her out, feeling that was the sort of behaviour expected of a gentleman who was courting a lady. He had not yet admitted to himself he would even consider marrying Henrietta.

But her very apparent indifference to him made his great democratic gesture seem as nothing. He felt she might at least have shown some awareness of his great condescension. Since he had come into the title, he had been toadied to quite dreadfully and, not having had a very high opinion of women at any time, he assumed he had only to smile at one of them for her to flutter eagerly in his direction.

Through the snow, he saw the blurred image of an inn sign and turned into the courtyard. The servants would need to join them. The weather was too bad to allow them to risk trying to get to London by themselves.

It proved to be little more than a hedge tavern, but the landlord looked clean and decent and was overjoyed at a chance of entertaining members of the quality.

The little inn was empty of other customers because of the terrible weather, and soon they were seated by the tap in front of a roaring fire, drinking hot punch and feeling like a band of explorers who had come down from the glaciers. The servants were ensconced in the kitchen.

Mr Clifford thought it all very romantic. He sat close to Josephine on a high-backed wooden settle beside the fire. She had placed her ruin of a bonnet over the poker to dry. Her springy chestnut hair shone with threads of gold in the firelight.

Mr Clifford looked cautiously around. The earl was telling Miss Bascombe about one of the famous peninsular battles. Lord Charles was telling Charlotte all about Gentleman Jackson's Boxing Saloon, and Charlotte was listening to him with as much interest as if he were telling her the latest court gossip. Miss Hissop had fallen asleep.

Mr Clifford felt the time had come to declare his intentions. There was no need to ask little Miss Bascombe or Miss Hissop for permission. Their approval of him was all too evident. To compose himself and to find the right words, he stood up with his back to the fire. He would take Josephine's hands, he decided, when no one was looking, and ask her what she thought about marriage. Yes, that would be a good start.

He went to sit down beside her again. But his breeches, his new leather breeches, had dried onto him like a second skin and refused to sit down when he did. He let out a cry of agony and slid down onto the floor.

In vain did he try to get up. Lord Charles and the Earl of Carrisdowne came over and hoisted him to his feet. But the wretched breeches seemed to be getting tighter by the minute. Mr Clifford was now very white about the face and looked on the point of fainting.

'It's those cursed breeches,' said Lord Charles. 'You'll need to get 'em off.'

'Shhh!' said Mr Clifford feebly. 'Ladies present.' He swayed, and the earl caught him just as he collapsed in a dead faint.

'Ladies,' said the earl, 'Mr Clifford is suffering badly from constriction. You must leave the room until we attend to him.'

The landlord was summoned and he offered his own parlour as sanctuary for the ladies. They woke Miss Hissop, and then they all left the room.

'Now, lay him down on the floor,' said the earl, 'and let's get these things off him.'

But the buttons could not be moved. 'Cut them off,' said Lord Charles. 'It's the only thing to do. He's turning blue about the mouth.'

'When I was a boy,' said the earl, producing a penknife, 'I used to see ladies get into this coil through too much tight lacing.' He cut the buttons and then had to saw the leather of the breeches on either side while Lord Charles held burning feathers under Mr Clifford's nose.

The landlord came in with a pewter bowl

144

filled with snow, and they pressed some of it to the back of Mr Clifford's neck. He slowly recovered and then sat up clutching his head.

'Easy,' said the earl. 'You had better wrap you nether limbs in a blanket, Guy. We had to send the ladies from the room.'

'And I was just on the point of proposing,' said Mr Clifford dizzily.

'Drink some brandy,' urged the earl, 'and then let us discuss the matter of marriage while the ladies are absent.' He waited while his brother hoisted Mr Clifford back onto the settle and gave him a glass of brandy.

The colour returned to Mr Clifford's cheeks. 'Oh, my breeches,' he mourned.

'Never mind your demmed breeches,' drawled Lord Charles. 'My dear brother is about to deliver himself of a jaw-me-dead about the folly of marrying into a shop.'

'I was merely going to point out the folly of leaping into marriage before you have properly courted the girl,' said the earl. 'It is not fair to Miss Archer. What do you know of each other? Snatched conversations in a busy shop, one dinner, and one disastrous outing.'

Mr Clifford scratched his head. 'Seems to me it doesn't really matter,' he said, puzzled. Can't say I've felt like this before. Never wanted to *cherish* any of the others, if you know what I mean.'

'Nonetheless, you must admit you were about to be hasty.'

'Perhaps you have the right of it,' said Mr Clifford reluctantly. 'I'm certainly not going to propose now, not with a blanket wrapped around me. So long as you're not going to mess things up for me, Rupert, I don't mind waiting.'

'I never messed things up, as you put it, for you before,' said the earl. 'As I recall, you were deuced glad I came to the rescue.'

'Well, it ain't that I'm not grateful,' said Mr Clifford. 'But it don't follow I'm naturally about to make another mistake.'

'And what about you, Charles?' demanded the earl, fixing his brother with a steely look.

'Oh, I don't mind biding my time,' said Lord Charles airily. 'Early days yet.'

The earl looked at his younger brother suspiciously. It was hard to tell half the time what Charles was really thinking.

'And what about you?' rejoined Lord Charles. 'Never say you are squiring Miss Bascombe for the sole purpose of keeping an eye on the pair of us. Too Gothic.'

'I enjoy Miss Bascombe's company, that is all,' said the earl repressively. Privately he

146

thought things were moving too fast and was glad he had dissuaded Guy from proposing. What did they know of these women?

When Henrietta was next to him, the earl found it very hard to think clearly. But when she was not, all of his old caution and all his distaste for her manner of earning her living returned in full force.

The ladies were brought back in. Modesty forbade them from mentioning the reason for Mr Clifford's constriction. It was politely assumed his cravat had been too tight, and eyes were delicately averted from the blanket wrapped about his nether limbs.

The landlord appeared to say that the snow had changed to rain and that the roads were clearing fast. Soon they were able to arrange themselves in the carriages with rugs over their heads to make the journey back.

Because of the miserable weather, it was a silent journey home, the earl breaking the silence only once to beg Henrietta to attend a play with him the followng evening.

Henrietta accepted, feeling as if spring had come at last. She felt warm and elated. Here was more proof that the earl had forgiven her for being in trade; for an outing to the playhouse was even better than a picnic. He would be seen with her before the eyes of society.

As the carriages with their sodden occupants turned into Half Moon Street, the sun burst through the ragged clouds, gilding the cobbles and shining on the golden pineapple above the door of Bascombe's.

Josephine and Charlotte began to chatter like schoolgirls as they unwrapped themselves from the wet rugs. Lord Charles and Mr Clifford were teasing them both and saying that if they had not both died from rheumatism by the morrow, they would take them driving at the fashionable hour. The earl jumped down and, after helping Miss Hissop, lifted Henrietta down from his carriage.

She felt the strength of his hands at her waist and noticed the evident reluctance with which he released her when he had set her on the ground. He raised her hand to his lips. 'Tomorrow?' he asked.

'Yes, tomorrow,' said Henrietta huskily. He kissed her hand. He said, 'The play begins at seven, but most of the ton do not attend until nine.'

'I have never been to the playhouse before,' said Henrietta. 'I should like to see the play from the beginning.'

'It is Shakespeare's *A Winter Tale*. The performance is said to be very fine. I shall call for you at six thirty.'

148

He bowed and jumped up into his carriage.

Mr Clifford and Lord Charles were standing on the pavement laughing and joking with Josephine and Charlotte. Miss Hissop stood by the shop door, waiting for Henrietta to unlock it and wondering why the girl was still standing on the pavement, her hands to her lips, watching the earl drive away.

CHAPTER NINE

The next evening as Henrietta was preparing to go to the theatre, Josephine and Charlotte sat on their beds to watch her dress for the great occasion.

Both girls had returned from the park, much elated at the success of their outing. The sun had shone, the afternoon had been fine, and it was evident from their report that both Mr Clifford and Lord Charles had gone out of their way to present them to many leading members of the ton.

'And that must surely mean marriage,' ended Charlotte. 'Lord Charles's whole manner toward me is not that of a man who is seeking an idle affair.'

'Yes,' agreed Henrietta. 'Both Lord Charles and Mr Clifford appear to behave very prettily.'

'We *all* have beaux now,' said Josephine.

'Not I,' said Henrietta, twisting this way and that in front of the looking glass.

'But Carrisdowne *is* your beau,' protested Charlotte.

'I am merely allowing Lord Carrisdowne to squire me to the play because it keeps Bascombe's in fashion.'

'Dear Henrietta,' said Josephine tentatively, 'I should not like to think you were encouraging Lord Carrisdowne merely to promote the happiness of myself and Josephine. Although you say it is all for the sake of the shop, I know you have our welfare at heart. *I* think Lord Carrisdowne is a dangerous-looking man. So fierce! You must not play with his affections.'

'His affections!' laughed Henrietta. 'He does not have any.' Then she remembered that kiss and blushed.

She still did not quite trust the earl or his interest in her. She sometimes suspected him of playing a deep game, suspected him of staying close to her so that he might find a way of alienating the affections of Lord Charles and Guy from Josephine and Charlotte.

'I confess we owe you much,' said Charlotte. 'Never did I think I should have such a wonderful time. I do not even feel tired anymore. But *if*, as you say, you are not interested in Lord Carrisdowne, why did you get the dressmaker to work all last night and today to supply you with that very splendid ensemble in time for the theatre?'

Henrietta was wearing a dress of spotted India muslin with puckered sleeves, the front richly ornamented with silver trimming and lace. Over the dress she wore a Persian robe of rich-figured amber sarcenet, made without sleeves and loose from the shoulders. A rouleau of silver muslin bound her glossly curls. The dress had armlets of gold, studied with paste rubies, and was confined under the bosom with a golden girdle.

'I felt I must look my best,' explained Henrietta. 'I am by way of being an advertisement for Bascombe's. Besides, Miss Hissop has new finery, and *she* is not going to the play.'

Henrietta had felt obliged to order new clothes for Miss Hissop. Unthinkable that she, Henrietta should spend so much on just one gown when Poor Miss Hissop was in such dire need of new clothes.

Miss Hissop was proudly wearing the first of several gowns Henrietta had ordered for her. It was a soft dove-grey velvet, and Miss Hissop had cried tears of gratitude after she had tried it on, saying that it was so very beautiful she had a good mind to change the instructions for her funeral and request that she be buried in it.

Although the profits from the confectioner's were to be divided equally among the four of them, all had agreed to live as frugally as possible, saving all they could for the girls' dowries and Miss Hissop's retirement. But when the others had insisted that Henrietta's theatre gown should be paid for from their joint savings, she in turn had been equally insistent that all their clothes in that case should be charged to the profits before they were divided up.

Henrietta had become very fond of Josephine and Charlotte. Although both girls were older than she, Charlotte being twenty-two and Josephine twenty, Henrietta at nineteen felt older than they. If only she could keep Lord Carrisdowne amused and interested, then Mr Clifford and Lord Charles might propose to the girls very soon.

Her hopes for them took predominance over her own desires. The earl was an enigma, but he was an intelligent man and courteous company.

Having convinced herself that all her excitement at the prospect of spending an evening in his company was dictated by her delight in being shown to society in such exalted company, Henrietta was quite unprepared for her own reactions when she saw him again.

Esau came shuffling reluctantly up the stairs to scratch at the door and announce that 'him' was below.

The earl was standing in the middle of the shop in black evening dress and diamonds. Henrietta came down the stairs so softly that he was not aware of her approach. She stood looking at him for a brief moment, her heart doing a somersault. He looked so very grand, so very masculine, the cascading white muslin of his cravat setting off the hard firm lines of his tanned face. His black evening breeches were moulded to his legs, showing all the strength of the muscles in his thighs. He looked cool and remote and every inch the aristocrat.

Why does he bother with me? thought Henrietta in sudden panic. Why?

The earl turned and saw her. A smile softened the harsh lines of his face. Those black eyes of his that gave so very little away studied Henrietta in silence. Then he said, 'You look like a fresh rose with the dew on it, sparkling, untouched, not yet full-blown.'

'A pretty compliment, my lord.' Henrietta avoided his intense gaze. 'Shall we go?'

The press of carriages as they approached the Theatre Royal, Drury Lane, was so great, and Henrietta was so anxious not to miss the beginning of the play that they alighted from the carriage a few streets away and walked to the theatre.

A covey of bloods came barrelling along the street, and the earl pulled Henrietta tightly against his side and swung her away from them so that she wouldn't be roughly knocked. That brief contact made her feel dizzy. It was weak and humiliating to have such violent physical reactions to a man who did not seem too much moved by the same contact.

There were only two playhouses in London: the Theatre Royal, in Drury Lane, and the Haymarket Theatre. It was a sad change from the days of Queen Elizabeth and King James I when London, then only a tenth of its present size, contained seventeen theatres. But the two remaining playhouses were enormous. Old people said the acting was better in their young days because there were more schools for actors then, and the theatres were so small that the natural voice could be heard and the natural expression of the features seen, and therefore rant and distortion were unnecessary.

As Henrietta and the earl approached the Theatre Royal, they saw the soldiers stationed at the doors in case of riots, and as they drew nearer they were pestered by women trying to sell them oranges and boys selling playbills.

Once inside, Henrietta was overawed by the size, the height, the splendour, and the beauty of the theatre. The pit was capable of holding a thousand people. Above it, on three sides, rose four tiers of boxes supported by thin iron pillars and above them, two galleries, the higher at such a distance that anyone taking a place there had to be content with the spectacle, for it was impossible to hear the dialogue. The theatre was decorated in colours of blue and silver and the whole illuminated with chandeliers of cut glass.

The people in the galleries were very noisy as Henrietta and the earl took their places in his box. They were whistling and calling to the musicians and passing the time waiting for the play to begin by throwing orange peel at the audience in the pit.

Although both pit and galleries were already full, the earl explained that the lower side boxes, of which theirs was one, did not begin to fill up until toward the middle of the first act because, he told her, that part of the audience considered themselves too fashionable to come on time, and in any case came to see the other fashionables and to be seen themselves rather than to listen to the play.

He did not tell her that the front boxes—those facing the stage—did not fill until halfway through the play, when they would be swarming with prostitutes and the men who came to meet them. There had been a move to prevent prostitutes from entering the theatre, and men had been placed at the doors during the previous year to keep them out. But, alas for the fashions of the Regency! It was so hard to tell lady from prostitute! The whole plan was abandoned after two aristocratic ladies with highly painted faces and transparent muslin gowns had been marched off to the nearest roadhouse.

The play began. Henrietta watched the stage, and the earl watched Henrietta. He was fascinated by her rapt attention and the expressions that flitted across her face.

Noisy fights broke out during the play between the men in the front boxes vying for the custom of the prostitutes, but Henrietta did not even seem to notice. The play had lately been revived to display to advantage those two stars of the English stage, Mr Kemble and Mrs Siddons.

When the play was finally over—there were no intervals; they only had those on benefit nights—Henrietta heaved a sigh of pure delight.

'Do you wish to stay for the afterpiece?' asked the earl. 'It is *Don Juan.*'

'Oh, *yes,*' breathed Henrietta.

With all the candles blazing in the theatre, making it as bright as a sunny day, Henrietta became aware that many glasses were being turned curiously in the direction of their box.

Then, from the leering stares, the malicious giggles of the ladies, and the occasional loud remarks, the deeply humiliated Henrietta realized she was being regarded as Lord Carrisdowne's latest mistress. There were many jokes about the earl's 'sweet tooth.'

The earl looked thoughtfully at Henrietta's flushed and unhappy face, such a contrast to the childlike wonder that had transformed it during the play. He seemed to come to some decison.

He rose to his feet. 'Before the afterpiece begins,' he said, 'I should like you to meet someone. She is only two boxes away.'

'Who is it?' asked Henrietta nervously.

'My aunt, Lady Browne. She will not eat you.'

Henrietta was escorted by him from the box and soon found herself in the presence of Lady Browne, a terrifying-looking old dowager with a gimlet eye.

'Well, Carrisdowne?' she demanded. 'Never

say you have brought a lady to meet me at last.'

The earl performed the introductions.

'And how did you find the play, Miss Bascombe?' demanded Lady Browne.

'It was very fine. I—I thought it was wonderful, in fact. You see, I had never been to the playhouse before.'

'Such enthusiasm does you credit. I cannot abide these young misses who consider it fashionable to find everything a bore. Tell me, Carrisdowne, how does Emmeline?'

It transpired that Emmeline was the earl's mother. Henrietta listened while the earl discussed his mother's health. Then, 'We must leave,' he said. '*Don Juan* is about to begin.'

Henrietta curtsied low. Lady Browne took her hand and drew her face down to her own and kissed her on the cheek. 'I hope you never lose that fresh look,' she said. 'There are too many jaded women in London.'

The introduction and that kiss were noticed by many jealous female eyes. Miss Bascombe was *not* the earl's mistress, or he would not have introduced her to his aunt.

Lady Clara Sinclair clutched her fan so tightly that she broke one of the sticks. Until a few weeks ago, she had entertained hopes of a proposal from the earl. He had escorted her to the opera and had finally invited her to that dinner party where she had taken the role of hostess—although it was a role he had not asked her to assume.

She had believed his recent absence was due to his business affairs. Now it appeared all too plain that it was because of that sly Bascombe creature.

Spoiled and wilful, Lady Clara was used to getting anything she wanted. And she wanted the Earl of Carrisdowne. There must be some terribly simple way to drive that Bascombe woman out of London.

The old story of Don Juan was performed as a pantomine. It was a favourite spectacle everywhere. The London audience were delighted when the statue came to life, and the sound of his 'marble' footsteps always struck a dead silence through the theatre.

At last it was all over. The earl's coachman had battled and fought to find a place for the carriage at the front of the theatre.

They chatted about the play on the road home, Henrietta cheerful and animated and, for that short time, very much at ease in the earl's company.

Before he left her at the shop door, he wanted to kiss her very much indeed. But he knew in his mind that he had come to a point, to a crossroads, where he must decide what his own intentions were before making any more advances to her. He wanted her desperately. But always between him and his desire rose up the great wall of his pride.

After he had gone, Henrietta let herself into the sugar-smelling darkness of the shop. She twirled around, humming snatches of a popular ballad. Then she stretched her arms up to the ceiling. 'What a *wonderful* evening,' she cried.

Esau, crouching in the darkness of the shop, felt his heart sink. He could smell the stench of the workhouse in his nostrils and feel again the cut of the lash across his back. Something must be done to prevent Henrietta from marrying the earl.

'Something must be done to stop Carrisdowne from marrying that Bascombe shopgirl,' said Lady Clara.

Her brother, Lord Alisdair Sinclair, lounged in a chair opposite her in the sitting room of their family's town house. His feet in their muddy boots rested on a marble console table.

'Take some of my chums and break up her shop,' said Lord Alisdair. He was a dissipated young man who roamed the lower and dangerous parts of the town with his drunken friends.

'No,' said Lady Clara crossly. 'Carrisdowne would get to hear of it and you would be blamed, and then I should be suspected of having put you up to it. Everyone knows of my hopes of marriage to Carrisdowne.'

'That's 'cos you talk too much,' said her brother.

'Instead of sitting there criticizing me, you might put what's left of your brain to the problem and come up with something *sensible*.'

Lord Alisdair stretched and yawned. 'Begad,' he said, 'the simplest way is always the best. Smoke her out.'

'Smoke her out? She is not a *cobbler*.' It was considered prime sport among the bucks and bloods to blow cigar smoke into a cobbler's little closed stall where he slept during the night so that they might enjoy the jolly spectacle of seeing the cobbler come staggering out, gasping for breath.

'I mean, set fire to her shop.'

'And if someone sees you?'

'No one will see *me*. Don't do my drinking in Tothill Fields for nothing. Plenty of villains down there'd jump at the chance to do it for a golden boy.'

'Only a sovereign to get rid of that Bascombe?' Lady Clara smiled, a slow, catlike smile. 'The only bargain to be found, little brother, in these expensive days. Very well. Burn her out! Carrisdowne hasn't yet proposed, evidently, or we'd have heard of it, and without a place to stay she will need to return, even if temporarily, to where she came from. That will leave the field open for me.'

'And what if Miss Bascombe and her ladies perish in the fire?' Lord Alisdair fixed his sister with a beady eye.

'Dear Alisdair, what with pestilence, fires, riots and hangings, London is full of dead bodies. A few more won't make any difference. Besides, the Bascombe creature is in *trade*. She is not one of us. She is no more one of us than any of those wretches we saw being hanged at Newgate t'other week. Do not tell me you are become overnice in your feelings?'

'Not I, sis. Oh, no, not I.'

CHAPTER TEN

The next day Henrietta served the Duke of Gillingham with bergamot chips instead of apple salad and left the turtle soup to boil over on the kitchen fire.

The more she thought about the evening at the theatre, the more dazed she became with happiness. The great Earl of Carrisdowne was turning out to be her *friend*. She could hardly believe her good fortune. Perhaps, one day, he might even begin to entertain warmer feelings toward her. She was sure he had only kissed her because he had considered her far enough beneath him to accept such easy familiarities. But he had introduced her to his aunt. Miss Hissop, on hearing of this, had said he must have serious intentions, but Henrietta felt that was too optimistic a hope for the moment. It was enough that he liked and respected her. Her mind shied away from examining her own feelings too closely. The marriages of Josephine and Charlotte still held predominance in her thoughts and each mark of the earl's respect seemed to bring the realization of that ambition closer.

She had not slept very much the night before and so she was exhausted by the time the chores of the day were completed along with the lengthy preparations for the next.

By ten o'clock she was fast asleep.

By eleven o'clock, the other girls and Miss Hissop were asleep as well, while downstairs, in a makeshift bed in the back shop, Esau tossed and turned, plagued by uneasy dreams.

At two in the morning, Lord Alisdair's ruffians held a piece of brown paper smeared with syrup against the glass panes of the door. One of them tapped against the paper with a hammer until the glass broke. They gently lifted out the broken glass stuck to the paper and stuffed a pile of oily rags through the hole they had made so that the rags fell onto the floor of the shop. Then they lighted a torch and threw it in on top of the rags.

There were so many fires in London that had it not been for an amazing coincidence, Bascombe's might have been burned to the ground. Fires were usually caused by exploding coals or candles. Only the week before a gentleman had set the tail of his shirt afire by climbing into bed with his back to his bed candle. The flames from his blazing shirt had caught the bedcurtains, and, although the gentleman had escaped, his house had burned to the ground.

All the insurance companies had fire engines and firemen, but if you were not insured—and Henrietta was not—or if you had not paid up your premiums, then they would drive past without even stopping to watch the blaze.

There had been inventions for preventing fires, but they had come to nothing.

A Mr David Hartley had suggested lining every room with metal, and Lord Stanhope had invented a kind of mortar for the same purpose, but they were not adopted because no law was

164

passed to compel the adoption. Houses in London were built for sale, and the builder did not want to incur the expense of making them fireproof, because, if the house went on fire, then he would not be the one to be burned.

As far back as 1724, inventor Ambrose Godfrey had produced balls filled with chemicals that would extinguish a fire. The Royal Society of Arts even built a house in Marylebone fields to try out his invention. His devices were thrown into the burning rooms where they exploded, and the fire was successfully quenched. But it was a trade in England to put out fires, and 'All trades must live,' as the current motto went. So the firemen and the funeral directors got together, and when Godfrey or any of his friends tried to mount a ladder to throw one of his balls into a burning building, they simply pulled the ladder from under him, until the life of every person using them became endangered. And so that was the end of fire-extinguishing devices.

As Lord Alsidair's ruffians ran off down the street, coincidence in the form of the Earl of Carrisdowne turned the corner of Piccadilly onto Half Moon Street.

He had been playing cards at Watier's on Bolton Street and had persuaded himself that it was just as quick to walk home along Piccadilly and down Half Moon Street as it was to go via Berkeley Square.

He tried to ignore the little voice inside that kept telling him he was behaving like any love-smitten youth and was really hoping for some sign of Henrietta. Perhaps she might still be awake and working in the kitchen.

He saw the two dark figures running away, and then a tongue of flame leaped through the door of Bascombe's. Shouting for help, he ran toward the shop.

Esau awoke with a start. He always slept lightly. In the workhouse it had been a mistake to indulge in heavy sleep when even the skimpy rags might be stolen off your back. He smelled smoke. He faintly heard the earl's shout. He staggered to the door of the back shop and flung it open.

The pile of oil rags had blossomed into a sheet of flame. Esau screamed, a terrified animal scream.

Henrietta, almost as light a sleeper as Esau, leaped from bed and rushed down the stairs to the shop. Esau was standing helplessly, whimpering and wringing his hands.

'Water!' shouted Henrietta. 'Fetch water, Esau.'

And then a tall figure hurtled through the flames and fell onto the shop floor, rolling over and over to extinguish the greedy flames licking at his coat.

'Carrisdowne!' cried Henrietta. Galvanized into action, Esau ran to fetch water.

'Blankets,' rapped out the earl, jumping to his feet. 'Blankets, Miss Bascombe.'

'Esau's,' said Henrietta. 'The back shop.'

She ran into the back shop and snatched up Esau's blankets and then thrust the bundle at the earl. He threw them over the flames and then stamped on them, cursing as a tongue of flame singed the black silk of his breeches.

Esau staggered in with pails of water. 'More,' ordered the earl, snatching them from him.

'The curtains,' gasped Henrietta, for the pretty chintz curtains were ablaze. He threw the water over them and then ran about like a madman, stamping down the flames, kicking off bits of flaming rag that stuck to his shoes.

Esau came back with more water, and it was thrown on the dying blaze. The earl went with Esau this time to the scullery pump.

When they returned, Henrietta was beating down the remaining flames with a broom, unaware of the fact that she was clad in nothing but a flimsy nightdress and a frivolous frilly nightcap.

'That's it,' said the earl with satisfaction as the water he and Esau had brought doused the rest of the flames.

'Go upstairs to the cupboard on the landing and get more blankets for your bed, Esau,' said Henrietta. 'If the others are awake, tell them what happened.'

People in the street outside were clustering around the burned and shattered door. The earl took off his coat and put it around Henrietta's shoulders.

'Go away,' he snapped at the curious faces at the door.

One by one they drifted off. 'I shall send my servants round with some sort of door or piece of wood to keep you secure for the night,' said the earl.

'Oh, th-thank you,' whispered Henrietta, now shaking with shock.

There was a sooty smut on one cheek, and her large eyes were full of tears. He drew her gently into his arms and held her against his breast.

'It's all over,' he murmured against her hair. 'Do not cry. I shall take care of you.' He tilted her chin up. 'Smile. There is nothing to be afraid of.'

Henrietta gave him a watery smile. He kissed her gently on the mouth, feeling such a mixture of sweetness and passion that he forgot where he was.

The noise of female screams and exclamations coming down the stairs finally penetrated his brain, and he reluctantly freed his lips.

Miss Hissop burst into the room followed by Josephine, Charlotte, and Esau. They cried and exclaimed over the blackened mess of the room, hugged Henrietta, praised the earl for his bravery, and told Esau he was the best servant in London.

'So terrifying,' gasped Miss Hissop. 'We might have all been burned to a crisp, and then what would have happened to my funeral? Oh, to think all my dear funeral instructions might have been burned with me! Henrietta, my funeral instructions must from now on be lodged at the bank.'

The earl took a deep breath, and when all the exclamations and cries had died away, he bowed to Miss Hissop, and said, 'Miss Hissop, I shall call on Miss Bascombe in three days time. I would I could make it sooner, but I have matters to attend to. May I have your permission to see her alone? I have something very important to ask her.'

'Yes,' said Miss Hissop, startled into uttering only that one monosyllable.

Henrietta looked up at him as he raised her hands to his lips.

'I shall leave you now and send my servants

with something to board up the door for the rest of the night.'

'Bascombe's will not be opening for a few days,' said Henrietta ruefully. 'What a mess! But we shall come about. At least any orders for centrepieces are to be delivered next week, so I shall have time to make this shop sparkling again. Oh, and thank you for your advice. I have been unfashionable enough to start demanding money in advance.'

'Till Friday, then. At six o'clock,' he said, kissing first one hand and then the other.

'Friday,' echoed Henrietta softly.

'Now,' he said, turning to the others, 'I must report this fire to the authorities. It was set deliberately. I saw two men running away from the door of the shop.'

Miss Hissop let out a faint scream.

'Someone is jealous of your success. I suggest that in future Esau sleeps in the shop itself.'

After he had left, they all clustered around Henrietta. The earl quite obviously meant to propose to her. Would she accept?

And Henrietta, thinking of his handsome face, the touch of his lips, and the sweetness of his smile, gave a little gulp and said, 'Yes. Yes, I will. Yes, I *will* marry the Earl of Carrisdowne.'

They were so busy laughing and hugging her that they did not notice Esau creep sadly away, an Esau tortured with fears for his future now that his mistress was to wed.

The earl did not tell Mr Clifford or Lord Charles of his appointment with Henrietta, but both men heard about it when they visited the shop the next morning to find the door boarded up and a sign in the window saying that Bascombe's was temporarily closed because of fire.

Charlotte saw them at the window and let them in. The story of the fire had to be told again and again, and it was only at last that they learned how Carrisdowne had asked Miss Hissop's permission to call on Henrietta.

They set to with a will, helping the girls to clean the blackened floor and scrub the soot from the shelves, although Henrietta protested, saying that the maids, who were at work in the kitchen would help with the shop later. But it was all a novelty to Mr Clifford and Lord Charles. Each man was elated at the thought of Carrisdowne proposing to Henrietta.

They left late in the afternoon, saying that the next morning, the Thursday, they were setting out for Newmarket, and promising the girls that they would return as soon as possible.

When they had walked away from the shop, Lord Charles murmured, 'As soon as he pops the question, we'll pop ours. Let him go first.'

'Don't see why we should wait,' said Mr Clifford. 'Let's go back now and ask 'em.'

'Oh, let Rupert have all the fun of first proposal. He's not such a bad old stick.'

'Hope it's going to be all right,' said Mr Clifford. 'When's he seeing her? Friday? Whoever heard of a man proposing on a Friday?'

Friday was considered an unlucky day in England. Friday was the usual day for executions, the idea being that it gave the condemned time to travel to heaven on the Saturday and get through the pearly gates by the Sunday. No one ever married on a Friday, and sailors would not put to sea on that unlucky day, even if the winds were favourable.

'It will be all right,' said Lord Charles soothingly. 'Forgot to ask Charlotte...little Miss Bascombe's going to accept him, isn't she?'

'Yes, definitely. Told them all she was.'

'There you are! Never believed that stuff about Fridays anyway.'

Esau worked and listened to the chatter in the shop. He worked and worried. There must be some way to stop Henrietta from marrying. He was to be paid on the tenth of June. Once he had his wages, he would feel more secure. Somehow matters must be delayed until then.

He felt sure the minute Henrietta accepted the earl's proposal, she would promptly close down the business. Even Esau knew it was unthinkable that the great Earl of Carrisdowne should have a fiancée in trade.

A busy time made the hours fly past until Friday. The carpenter hung a new door, and Henrietta herself repainted the shop walls.

On Friday Bascombe's opened again, but there were very few customers, nobody thinking they could get on their feet again so very quickly.

The day passed very slowly for Henrietta. She planned to close the shop as early as half past five.

A coachman and carriage had been hired to take the girls, Miss Hissop, and Esau for a long drive in the park while the important proposal was going on.

Miss Hissop had protested strongly, saying that Henrietta must be chaperoned, but Henrietta said that, being the owner of Bascombe's, it was pefectly correct to see the earl alone.

The shop was closed at last. The rest left in the hired carriage to take the air. By six, Henrietta was sitting by the window in a pretty gown of sprigged muslin, heart beating hard, waiting for her lord to come.

The little French gilt clock up on the shelf chimed six. She waited with increasing impatience. What if he did not come? What if that great pride of his had persuaded him that to propose to a shopgirl was folly? And if he changed his mind, what then would become of Josephine and Charlotte?

Would he never come? Henrietta began to pace up and down. The others would not be back until after seven. But the precious minutes were ticking away.

She heard footsteps in the street outside and rushed to the window.

Lady Clara Sinclair stopped outside the shop on the arm of a thin, dissipated youth. Henrietta did not know that the youth was Lord Alisdair.

'Pity it did not burn properly' came Lady Clara's voice. 'You must have hired fools.'

'Try again another time,' drawled the young man laconically.

They moved off. They had not seen Henrietta because she had moved behind the curtain as soon as she had recognized Lady Clara.

She sat down suddenly. So that was who was behind the attempt to burn the shop.

Where was the earl? *He* would know what to do. If he had changed his mind, if he had decided he did not want her, then she would indeed feel friendless. Only the earl could advise her as to how to go about bringing aristocrats like Lady Clara into court.

How very beautiful, how very fashionable, Lady Clara had looked. How could the earl look at *her*, Henrietta Bascombe, shopkeeper, when there were so many beauties about?

And then she heard his firm step. She knew instinctively it was he. Henrietta stood up, her hands clasped to her bosom, her heart in her eyes.

CHAPTER ELEVEN

The earl would have been on time for his appointment with Henrietta if he had not met Esau, who was sitting forlornly on the steps of the Grosvenor Chapel.

Esau had asked to be set down, saying he did not feel like going for a drive. Miss Hissop, cross that their male servant should not wish to accompany them, pointed out that the doors of the church were closed.

But Esau, showing a rare streak of stubbornness, insisted, and Miss Hissop, who secretly admired Esau's religious fervour, gave in.

The earl recognized the servant by his familiar squint and red plush livery. Esau was small for his age, and he looked a sad little figure sitting on the church steps.

'Why are you not in the shop?' asked the earl, stopping in front of him.

'Mistress sent us away,' said Esau. 'The rest of the ladies is gone to the park for a drive.'

The earl smiled with pleasure at the prospect of seeing Henrietta alone. He was about to take his leave when he noticed large tears were standing out in Esau's eyes, making the squint more pronounced.

'What ails you?' he asked gently. 'It is the shock from the fire, no doubt.'

Esau solemnly shook his head. The reason for his tears was because he was sure the devil had sent the earl. Esau had long debated telling the earl some lie so that the proposal would never take place. He had gone to the church for comfort and had quite resolved to behave himself and accept the inevitable. But here was the earl, and here was the opportunity. Still, he hesitated, but the noise and the filth of the dreaded workhouse rose before his eyes.

'I am in sore distress about mistress,' he said, enunciating slowly and clearly.

'Miss Bascombe? What is the matter with

Miss Bascombe?' The earl's voice was sharp with anxiety.

'She's a good lady,' said Esau, 'and I don't like to see her going on the way she does. She would do anything for money, she says, not wanting to be poor again, but it goes against my pinsipulls.'

'What goes against your principles?'

'Her selling herself,' said Esau in a low voice. 'First to the Duke of Gillingham, then to Mr Brummell, and now she's going to sell herself to you.'

'Do you know what you are saying?'

Esau quailed before the blaze of anger on the earl's face. He, Esau, might quickly be found out in his lie and lose his employ, but he was shrewd beyond his years and knew that in their heart of hearts most gentlemen were prepared to believe the worst of the ladies. He had often returned to the servants' pub to keep up with the gossip and had heard the servants faithfully repeating their masters' cynical opinions about Lady this and Miss that.

'Yes,' said Esau. I've lied now he thought, and may God forgive me, but I'm going to make this a really big one. Aloud, he added, 'I would give her my wages if I thought it would stop her. I would work for *nothing.*'

A red mist of anger rose before the earl's

eyes. He did not want to believe Esau, but why should this child-servant lie to him? What did he really know of Henrietta Bascombe except the little that she herself had told him, and that very little had included her statement to him that she would do anything for money. Besides, she had gone into trade.

Esau knelt at the earl's feet and clutched the hem of his coat. 'Leave her alone, my lord,' he sobbed. 'She's good reelly.'

The earl jerked his coat hem from Esau's grasp. 'You no doubt think you have done me a favour,' he grated. 'But you are a disloyal servant.'

Esau shrank away from him and put up his hand to ward off the expected blow.

My world has fallen in ruins, thought the earl bitterly, and here I stand berating a child! He gave Esau a curt good-bye and strode off back the way he had come.

Esau dried his eyes on his sleeve. At least the earl would not be going to Bascombe's to keep that appointment.

But the earl was too furious, hurt, and sick to let matters rest. Instead of going into his house, he walked on past it, turned down Park Lane, along Curzon Street, and onto Half Moon Street.

He kept remembering her saying she would

do anything for money. She was no better than an abbess, no doubt renting Charlotte and Josephine out to the highest bidders. And not content with that, she had nearly trapped *three* of London's most eligible gentlemen into unsuitable marriages. He could only be glad that Guy and Charles were safely on the way to Newmarket.

He hammered on the shop door.

The light died out of Henrietta's eyes when she saw the expression on his face.

'Are we alone?' he demanded harshly.

'Y-yes,' faltered Henrietta.

He stood looking down at her, at the delicate pink of her cheeks, the softness of her mouth, and the swell of her bosom under her gown.

The shop had not yet been cleared of sweetmeats, cakes, jellies, and fruit. She looked as edible and delectable as one of her confections. The shop glowed with colour. There was a sweet smell of sugar and spice.

He pulled her roughly into his arms and crushed her mouth under his own. She returned his kiss eagerly, sweetly, and with newfound passion, and it was only after a few dazed moments that she realized how much he was punishing her mouth and that one expert hand had slid inside the neck of her dress to find her breasts.

Alarmed and shocked, she pushed him away with all her strength. Breathing heavily as if he had been running, he stood back, his black eyes sparkling with contempt.

'How much?'

Henrietta put a shaking hand up to her bruised mouth. 'I beg your pardon, my lord,' she said faintly.

'I said, how much?' he demanded. 'How much did you get from Gillingham and Brummell? You no doubt set your favours high. Well, madam, I am prepared to meet your price. I ask you again. How much?'

Henrietta took a few steps back from him until her back was against the polished wood of the counter.

'I do not know what you are talking about,' she whispered.

'I am offering to set you up as my mistress,' he said. 'You may come with me in the morning to my lawyers, and we shall arrange the terms. I cannot promise to keep that harem of yours as well, but no doubt they are experienced enough by now to look after themselves.'

'No!' cried Henrietta, white to the lips. 'You cannot mean it. You took me to the theatre, you introduced me to your aunt. You have been drinking!'

'I shall apologize to my aunt, and, no, I have

not been drinking. I have never been more sober in my life. You are a pretty baggage, Henrietta, and 'fore God, you still manage to look the picture of innocence. Come here!'

Anger rose up in Henrietta, suffocating anger. 'Get out!' she cried.

'Why?' His voice was cold, mocking. 'I am very rich. Rich enough to purchase anything *you* have to offer.'

'Get away!' said Henrietta shrilly, as he took a step nearer. 'You *disgust* me.'

'Oh, hoity-toity, miss. I never like bargaining. Is this how you put up your price?'

Henrietta felt beside her on the counter. Her hand encountered the thin stem of a tazza which held a gooseberry jelly. Henrietta had been proud of that jelly. She had added a little colouring to it. It was as green as grass, as green as jealousy.

As the earl took another purposeful step toward her, she raised the tazza and flung the contents full in his face.

'Hellcat!' he shouted, wiping green jelly from his face. 'I'll have you for that!'

Henrietta went completely insane with anger. As she darted about the shop, as he tried to catch her, she threw everything at him she could lay her hands on—tarts, crystallized fruit, wet confects, dry confects, cream cakes, and followed it all up by hurling a whole regiment of marzipan soldiers at his head.

'Be damned to you,' he shouted, blinded by cream and pastry. He scrubbed the mess from his face and strode to the door, opened it, and marched out into the street.

A large apple pie caught him right on the back of the head.

He hailed a passing hack and climbed in.

Henrietta sat down amid the wreck of her confectionery, amid the wreck of her dreams, and cried her eyes out. She was still sitting there, sobbing, when Charlotte, Josephine, and Miss Hissop came back.

Bitterly she sobbed out her tale of the earl's iniquities. Josephine and Charlotte began to cry as well. There was no doubt in their minds that Mr Clifford and Lord Charles had the same low ideas about *them*. Just like Mr Clifford and Lord Charles, the earl had *appeared* to show Henrietta every respect and attention before this last terrible visit. The stigma of being in trade weighed heavily on their souls. It stopped Josephine and Charlotte from thinking clearly. The attentions of such great personages as Lord Charles and Mr Clifford had always seemed too good to be true.

Esau crept quietly in and set about clearing up the mess. He felt a mean and evil person.

He was sure now that God would punish him. In fact, he became so sure of the divine wrath about to be visited on his head that he finally threw down his cleaning cloth into the bucket and sat down on the floor and added his sobs and wails to the general lamentation.

Henrietta was the first to dry her eyes. 'London is a wicked and evil place,' she said. 'I was overambitious in setting up business here. Thank goodness we have made enough money so that we may close up here and open somewhere else.'

'Where?' sobbed Josephine.

'Bath,' said Henrietta. 'That's it! We'll go to Bath. I could not bear to stay here, knowing everyone considered us no better than doxies.'

'Could we not just go home?' ventured Miss Hissop.

'No,' said Henrietta. 'Josephine would be beaten, and there is not enough money yet to set up Charlotte for life. Esau must be taught the trade, and I must have a thriving business to turn over to him. He is a good and loyal servant.'

Esau rolled about the floor in an agony of guilt and remorse when he heard Henrietta's words. He had been so unused to any kindness in the past that it had never crossed his mind that she would make provision for his future at all, let alone such a magnificent offer.

Henrietta knelt down beside him. 'You take our troubles too much to heart. Do not cry, Esau. I really always wanted to go to Bath. And do you know, I don't care a fig for the Earl of Carrisdowne.'

Esau stopped crying and sat up. 'Do you mean that?' he asked eagerly.

'Yes, Esau,' said Henrietta, clenching her fists. 'I hate that man as I've never hated anyone in the whole of my life. Oh, and there is another reason why we must leave.' She told them about Lady Clara. 'So you see,' she ended, 'there is no point in trying to take her to court. It would only be my word against hers— and what judge is going to prosecute Lady Clara Sinclair? Let us get away from this wicked city before it kills us!'

Mr Clifford and Lord Charles had gone to Newmarket to see Lord Charles's horse, Calamity, run in the races. They had not wanted to leave London, but it had been learned that Lord Charles's jockey was a trifle overweight, and although he was reported to be stewing between two featherbeds to get down to the right weight, Lord Charles felt he should be there in person to make sure the man was trying hard enough.

Mr Clifford had a bet of a thousand pounds on Calamity. It was the largest bet he had ever laid on anything. He hated leaving Josephine, but he was determined to be on the spot to assist Lord Charles in bringing about a successful race.

The horse won, Mr Clifford was considerably richer, and both men made their way back by easy stages to London. Life appeared very sunny and secure. Not for one moment did they doubt that the earl and Henrietta would be engaged on their return. It was over a week since they had seen the girls, and so they decided to call at Half Moon Street first.

'That's deuced odd,' said Mr Clifford as they turned the corner from Piccadilly.

'What is?'

'Look! No golden pineapple. It's gone.'

'Probably taken it down to get it cleaned.'

They drove up to the door of the shop. The windows were shuttered and the door boarded up. A sign on the door proclaimed the shop was available to rent.

'Gone!' Lord Charles pushed back his beaver hat and scratched his head. 'They *can't* have gone.'

'Oh, I have it,' said Mr Clifford. 'You know what a high stickler Rupert is. He'll have got

Henrietta to close down immediately. He'd never stand for having his fiancée working in a shop.'

Lord Charles's face cleared. 'That's bound to be the reason. Let's go to Upper Brook Street immediately and offer our congratulations.'

Lord Carrisdowne, they were told in sepulchral tones, was in the study. They both breezed in and stopped short on the threshold. The earl was sitting in an armchair by the fire, a glass of brandy in his hand.

'Well, well,' he said, his voice slightly slurred, 'the lovers have returned, I can save you a visit to Bascombe's. Or perhaps you might have more success than I if you send your banker first.'

'What are you talking about, Rupert?' Lord Charles walked forward and stood over his brother.

'Miss Henrietta Bascombe,' said the earl in a weary voice, 'is a slut and a whore. To think she sat in this house and told me she would do anything for money, and I believed she was referring to the selling of confections. She meant herself, her favours, her body. Gillingham and Brummell have already had the pleasure. She is nothing more than an abbess, running a genteel brothel with a row of pretty

186

cakes as a smoke screen.'

'Never!' cried Lord Charles. 'I will not believe you. Charlotte Webster is the sweetest angel I ever beheld.'

'Then, go and ask them if you do not believe me.'

'But they've gone,' said Mr Clifford. 'Where have they gone? The shop is closed and shuttered and being offered for rent.'

The earl half closed his eyes as a great black wave of misery engulfed him. 'So,' he forced himself to say with a shrug, 'they have fled, and London is well quit of them.'

'Where did you come by this information? Surely Miss Bascombe never demanded money from you.'

'Her servant told me,' said the earl.

'Her *servant*!' Mr Clifford gave a scornful laugh. 'A boy she took from the workhouse. When did you ever pay any heed to servants' gossip?'

'The boy was crying with distress. I have no reason to doubt his word.'

'But what in heaven's name did Miss Bascombe say when you taxed her with it? Or did you simply walk away and never see her again?'

The earl shook his head as if to clear it. After all, what *had* she said? He remembered vividly the look of shock and betrayal on her face.

But *he could not be wrong.*

'She threw the contents of the shop at me.'

'At you? At one of the richest men in England? And yet you still believe her to be mercenary?'

'She was playing for higher stakes. She had expected an offer of marriage. I took her to the play and introduced her to Lady Browne in front of everyone. I asked Miss Hissop's permission to call on her.'

A mulish look settled on Mr Clifford's face. 'I don't believe it. I simply don't believe it for a minute. I think they are all as sweet and innocent as they appear. You're very high in the instep, Rupert, and I'm sure you readily believed the servant because you've always thought there was something dammed unladylike about them going into trade. Begad, man! I do not mind you bringing about the ruin of your own hopes, but to ruin my future and Charles's...'

The earl held up his hand. 'Enough! Did I not receive just such protestations before when each of you was about to form a mésalliance with a disreputable female?'

'When real love comes along,' said Lord Charles simply, 'there ain't any doubt about it. You *know*...that is if you ain't blinded with your own pride. Where have they gone?'

'I neither know nor care.'

'But you *must* know,' said Mr Clifford. 'When you saw Bascombe's was closed...'

'I did not know it was closed. I have hardly stirred from this house for a week.'

Mr Clifford and Lord Charles exchanged surprised glances over the earl's head. So he *had* been hit harder than they had thought! It seemed Lord Carrisdowne had at last been wounded in his heart as much as in his pride.

'We'll find 'em,' said Mr Clifford. 'They're bound to have told *somebody* where they were headed. You can't move a whole shop without someone stopping to ask where you're bound. And it isn't any use you trying to stop me, Rupert.'

'*I* shan't,' said the earl, filling his glass again. 'I'm weary of the whole thing. The pair of you may go to hell for all I care. Just never mention Henrietta Bascombe to me again!'

At first neither Lord Charles nor Mr Clifford could believe that the ladies of the confectionery had disappeared without a trace. They asked and asked. But no one had even found out where they had all come from in the first place.

As the days passed into weeks, and the Earl of Carrisdowne appeared at fewer and fewer fashionable functions, Mr Clifford and Lord Charles became moody and depressed. Lord

Charles saw as little of his brother as possible, and Mr Clifford, seeing the earl in the street one day, pointedly crossed over to avoid him.

The earl tried to forget that scene in the confectioner's. But in the middle of restless, sleepless nights, Henrietta's shocked face would rise up to haunt him. The little voice, which at first had nagged at him that he should not have listened to Esau, gradually became a shout. He could have gone and taxed Brummel or Gillingham and asked them about their relations with Henrietta, but he shrank from doing so. They would either confirm his worst fears, or, if the girl proved to be innocent, his very questions might lead both men to think her a jade.

Lady Clara had been persistent, sending letters and presents. He had burned the letters and returned the presents. Finally he had become tired of finding her 'passing just by chance' when he left the house and had given her a cruel set-down.

As the longing to see Henrietta became stronger and stronger, as he became more convinced he had damned her without a hearing, he became determined to find her. But inquiries at livery stables and coaching inns drew a blank. It was as if there had never been a Bascombe's, as if Henrietta, Josephine,

Charlotte, and Miss Hissop had never existed.

Lord Alisdair Sinclair returned home one evening to find his sister, Lady Clara, in tears.

'Haven't seen you cry this age,' he said. 'What's to do?'

'It is Carrisdowne,' said Lady Clara. 'He told me if he found me waiting outside his door again, he would need to order his servants to tell me to go away. He said...he said he was tired of being *annoyed* by me.'

'Never say you've been hanging about his doorstep like a trollop?'

'No, it was coincidence, nothing more,' lied Lady Clara, not meeting his eyes. 'I often walk down Upper Brook Street on my way to the park.'

Lord Alisdair wondered whether to point out that his sister always went to Hyde Park in the carriage and walked as little as possible but decided against it. Lady Clara's temper could be vicious.

'Well,' he said, 'that's the way of it. He don't want you. May as well cast your eye elsewhere. You've ruined a whole Season. Now we're all off to Brighton, you'll be able to put him from your mind.'

'No,' said Lady Clara mutinously. 'He loved

me once. I am convinced he will love me again.'

'Don't look like it.'

'It's that Bascombe woman.'

'Can't be. No one's seen hide nor hair of her. Must have got a fright after the fire.'

'Toby Miles said t'other day that Carrisdowne had emerged from the confectioner's covered in cream, and before he could get into a hack, a pie came sailing out and struck him on the back of the head.'

'Did it now,' grinned Lord Alisdair. 'I'd give a monkey to have seen that—the great and stately Carrisdowne getting his comeuppance. It looks, then, as if Miss Bascombe took against him, doesn't it? I mean, you don't go around shying pastry at someone you respect.'

Lady Clara tapped her foot impatiently. 'Listen! It is no secret that Carrisdowne's servants are trying to find out where the Bascombe creature has gone to. He must be obsessed with the woman.'

'You are all about in your upper chambers, sis. Leave Carrisdowne be. You will have gallants aplenty in Brighton.'

'*I want Carrisdowne,*' said Lady Clara shrilly, reminding her brother forcefully of the days when they had both been in the nursery and baby Clara had wanted one of his toys.

'You can't have him,' he said, 'and let that

be an end to it.'

'Even you have deserted me,' said Lady Clara, beginning to sob again.

He looked at her impatiently. There was little room in his weak and selfish heart for love or affection, but what little there was, he reserved for his sister.

'Don't cry,' he sighed. 'I shall find the Bascombe woman. I'll let Carrisdowne find her for me. Our servants will be given instructions to ask his servants about his movements. As soon as he shows any signs of leaving town, we shall follow him. But how we are going to ruin La Bascombe is another matter.'

'Find her,' said Lady Clara, drying her eyes, 'and I shall think of something.'

CHAPTER TWELVE

Although still one of the most beautiful towns in England, Bath had seen better days. When the great Beau Nash had acted as master of ceremonies, he had made the Bath assemblies as exclusive as Almack's. He had ruled with a rod of iron. Ladies who turned up at his assemblies not dressed according to his rigid standards were turned out. At the end of his life he had become helpless and poor and had died neglected and miserable. The inhabitants of Bath then erected a statute to this man they had suffered almost to starve.

His loss was felt keenly. Only a short time before Henrietta's arrival, two ladies of quality had quarrelled in the ballroom. The rest of the company took part, some on one side and some on the other. Beau Nash was gone, and they stood in no awe of his successor. They became outrageous, and a real battle royal took place, and the floor of the ballroom was strewn with caps, lappets, curls and cushions, diamond pins and pearls.

The town was full of cardsharpers and adventurers and it had more of death's advance guard than anywhere else in Britain as the sick and self-indulgent filled the pump room to take the waters.

Henrietta had been lucky in securing the lease of a shop in the centre of the town. With it went the apartments above so that they each had a bedroom and a cozy parlour.

Although she herself was regarded as highly unfashionable, Henrietta's confectionery was not. Her cakes and confections insured her success, and so long as Miss Bascombe and her ladies remembered their place and did not try to attend any of the assemblies, then society was pleased to give her its custom.

Henrietta was disappointed. She had hoped to provide Josephine and Charlotte with some social life. But the only men who seemed interested in any of them were seedy adventurers prepared to marry into a profitable business.

Josephine and Charlotte appeared resigned to their fate, Esau was receiving a full training in the making of confectionery from Henrietta, and Miss Hissop enjoyed their unadventurous life of hard work and sedate walks.

Henrietta marvelled at her friends' seemingly cheerful demeanours. She herself kept as busy as possible, but there was always a dull ache at her heart, always an irrational surge of hope when she saw a tall black-haired man at a distance. The most bitter thing she had to live with was the realization that she had fallen in love with the Earl of Carrisdowne, and though her mind daily lectured her emotions on their folly, there was nothing she could seem to do to alleviate the hurt and longing.

The sight of the earl's sister, Lady Sarah, sitting in a corner of the shop, wolfing cakes and sweetmeats, did nothing to help. Despite her plump appearance and fat cheeks, Lady Sarah had the earl's black eyes and high-bridged nose.

Henrietta knew the earl would be furious at

his sister eating so many cakes, but Henrietta could hardly turn her out of the shop.

And then one day, the Dowager Countess of Carrisdowne accompanied Lady Sarah on one of her visits. From their raised voices, Henrietta learned that Lady Sarah was supposed to have been visiting her music teacher all the times she was actually in the confectioner's.

'So this is where you go,' demanded the countess, black eyes snapping, 'and I would not have found out except I met that music teacher of yours in the street and asked him why he did not call at our house to give you lessons. He said you had had one lesson of him, and then had given him a letter, supposed to have come from me, cancelling the rest of the lessons.'

The countess waved an imperious hand and summoned Henrietta. 'I believe you are in charge of this establishment,' she said.

'Yes, my lady,' replied Henrietta, who knew the countess by sight, having often seen her passing the shop, attended by her footman. She looked very like her son the earl, although her hair was snow-white.

'In future, I beg you, do not supply my daughter with any confections. Is that understood?'

'Yes, my lady,' said Henrietta meekly.

'I think it is ridiculous,' pouted Lady Sarah. 'Skinny ladies are not the fashion, as well you know, Mama.'

'A certain pleasing roundness is one thing,' said the countess acidly. 'Letting oneself become fat and spotty is quite another.'

'May I take your order, my lady?' asked Henrietta.

'No, you may not.' Then her harsh features softened. A sweet smile lighted up her face, reminding Henrietta painfully of her son. 'I do not mean to be angry with *you*, miss...'

'Miss Bascombe, if it please your ladyship.'

'Ah, of course, you are *Bascombe's*. Well, Miss Bascombe, I think it monstrous enterprising for such a young and obviously gently bred lady as yourself to make her own way in life. I always did admire spirit in a woman. But this silly girl of mine must be protected from herself. Nonetheless, I am giving a dinner in two weeks time—let me see, Friday the thirteenth—and would like you to send a centrepiece to my home. Nothing military. Something pretty will do very well. Do you know where I live?'

'Yes, my lady,' said Henrietta. 'The Royal Crescent, number 9.'

Henrietta had once walked past the house, drawn there by lovesickness, dreaming of seeing the earl arriving to call on his mother, although the gossips said he avoided Bath like the plague.

'You may send me your bill along with the centrepiece,' added the countess. 'I believe in settling my accounts promptly.'

'Dinner is at five—I do not believe in these newfangled hours—so have it to me by four in the afternoon at the latest. Come along, Sarah.'

Sarah trailed out miserably after her mother. They started arguing again as soon as they reached the street. Henrietta turned away to serve another customer and therefore did not hear the countess's threat. 'You are become unmanageable, Sarah. This is what befalls me for having a child so late in life. I am too weary to cope with your nonsense. I shall write to Rupert this day and tell him of your lies and of your visits to that confectioner's.'

The Earl of Carrisdowne had just returned from Brighton. He had been summoned there by the Prince Regent to join the round of pleasure. Brighton had been one frivolity after another. Lady Clara had been there, her hungry eyes following him round the room when he had attended one of the assemblies at the Ship Inn. He began to wonder whether she might not be a trifle unbalanced, and that thought made him gloomier than ever. It appeared a female would need to have more than a touch of madness to fall in love with *him*.

He set about making preparations to move to his estates. Mr Clifford and Lord Charles, who had also gone to Brighton, were still there. They had recovered some of their spirits, but they still shunned the earl.

How easily they seem to have forgotten, thought the earl. For his part, he was still plagued day and night by longing for Henrietta. The more he thought about her, the more bitterly ashamed he became of his easy belief in Esau's story. The Duke of Gillingham and his duchess had also been in Brighton. He had observed them closely, and it was forcefully brought home to him that the old duke had no interest in any female whatsoever—even his wife.

He sat down to deal with the post that had piled up in his absence, separating bills from invitations and invitations from personal letters.

He started by reading his personal correspondence first. There were various letters from relatives and one from his mother. He recognized her heavy seal. The one from his mother would no doubt contain more complaints about Sarah. He decided to leave it to the last.

When he finally opened it after snapping the heavy seal and reflecting his mother must have used one whole stick of wax, the word *Bascombe's* seemed to leap up out of the page. His hands shook slightly as he smoothed out the parchment and carefully read the letter.

In it, his mother, as usual, complained of Sarah's gluttony. She added that Sarah had been frequenting a confectioner's when she should have been at her music lessons. *Not that it is not an exceptionally respectable establishment,* the countess had written, *and the little lady who runs Bascombe's appears to be a superior type of person.*

Bath!

The earl slowly lowered the letter. Henrietta was in Bath.

A bare two days before the earl had discovered the whereabouts of the missing Miss Bascombe, Lord Alisdair Sinclair sat in a Brighton coffeehouse, nursing an aching head. He could not tell whether the damage had been done by last night's rack punch or last night's wine or last night's brandy.

A surly gentleman slumped down at the table beside him. Lord Alisdair raised red-rimmed eyes and looked into the unsavoury blue-jowelled features of the Honourable Toby

Miles. 'Under the weather, hey?' demanded Mr Miles with a grin.

Lord Alisdair averted his eyes with a shudder. Mr Miles's teeth had all been filed to points—the latest fashion among the bloods, who wanted to spit through their teeth like coachmen.

'Bad as that,' said Mr Miles. He fished in one of his large pockets. 'Try that. Set you right in no time at all.'

Lord Alisdair took the little bottle Mr Miles was holding out to him. His gaze sharpened as he read the legend BASCOMBE'S ELIXIR on the side.

'Where did you get this,' he asked as casually as he could.

'M'father sent me a dozen. Very old, m'father. In Bath to drink that filthy water. Got gout.'

'And he bought this in Bath?'

'Stand to reason, don't it? Bascombe is probably some apothecary or quack. Place is crawlin' with 'em.'

'There was a Bascombe's on Half Moon Street,' said Lord Alisdair, 'which sold an elixir.'

'Well, I wouldn't know that, would I?' demanded Mr Miles testily. 'Never go near the place if I can help it. No race meetings in

London; no prizefights neither.'

'And your father, has he been in London this year?'

'Not left Bath this twenty year past. Are you going to drink that stuff or aren't you. 'Cos if you ain't, I'll have it back.'

'No,' said Lord Alisdair, sliding the bottle into his own pocket. 'Take it later. Just remembered. Have an urgent appointment with my sister.'

Life had never been better for Esau. It was a warm August. Bath was bathed in sunlight. Henrietta appeared to have forgotten the earl, the business was flourishing, and he, Esau, was to have the honour of making the centrepiece for the Countess of Carrisdowne. At first he had hesitated, frightened of running into the earl. He made the excuse to Henrietta that he was frightened of Lord Carrisdowne, as only a frightful person would have treated Miss Bascombe so badly. Henrietta assured him the earl was not in Bath, and, from gossip she had overheard, was not likely to visit the place. He had said he detested the town.

Henrietta had drawn up the plans for the centrepiece, and Esau worked long days and nights over it. At last he had created Pan sitting by the toffee rushes playing his sugar pipe while shepherds and shepherdesses danced about. Sometimes his touch was still too clumsy, and Henrietta had to help him finish some of the figures, but most of it was all his own work, and he was very proud of it.

The only thing that marred his pleasure was that he had to deliver it on Friday the thirteenth. What could be more unlucky! But Henrietta said roundly that this fear of Friday was nothing more than an old superstition.

Henrietta decided to let Esau deliver the centrepiece alone. The sooner she forgot all about the Earl of Carrisdowne the better, and seeing members of his family would do nothing to help.

Esau set out to climb up the cobbled streets to the Royal Crescent, pushing the handcart with the centrepiece on it.

Like most religious people of his time, Esau was also deeply superstitious. Huge black thunderclouds were building up to the west, and the sky above was brassy. The farther he got from the shop, the more apprehensive he became. Thunder grumbled in the distance. Esau had an uneasy feeling he was being followed. From time to time, he stopped and turned about. It was always as if someone had just dived for cover before he was able to set eyes on him. The thundery air felt heavy with menace.

Despite the heat, Esau shivered in his plush livery.

Then he heard the light patter of footsteps behind him.

'Young man!' called a hoarse voice.

Esau turned about and let out a squawk of fright. A Gypsy woman was standing there in her black and red clothes. Her black hair was coarse and matted under a scarf decorated with gold coins. The fringed edges of her shawl rose and fell in the hot, damp wind.

'What do you want of me?' demanded Esau, backing away.

'It's Friday the thirteenth, Esau,' cackled the Gypsy.

'How do you know my name?'

'I know everything,' said the Gypsy. 'I know there is bad luck everywhere this day. If you do not accept my help, your pretty sweetmeats in that cart will be ruined.'

Esau rallied. 'Then, you don't know everything,' he said. 'This here is a centrepiece what I made myself.'

'You are a good boy, Esau, and I would help you. Let me sprinkle a little magic sugar over it and all will be well.'

Esau relaxed. If that's all she wanted to do, let her. A little sugar dusting wouldn't mar the centrepiece. And he would be shot of her.

'Oh, go ahead,' he said.

She took a silver sugar shaker out of her pocket. Esau gently parted the tissue paper wrapping, and the Gypsy shook the shaker over the centrepiece.

'Can I go now?' mumbled Esau.

'Go, and remember, you will thank me for my help before this day is over.'

She turned on her heel and strode away with long mannish strides. Esau picked up the handles of his cart and continued on his journey.

What a strange encounter! And yet, he felt happier as he quickened his pace to reach the Countess of Carrisdowne's before the storm broke. Thank goodness he had left early. It was only three-thirty.

Miss Hissop glanced nervously up at the sky as she walked in the parade gardens. So kind of dear Henrietta to allow her so much free time, but it looked as if it might rain. She glanced at the watch pinned to her bosom. Five o'clock. Perhaps just a look at the river and then she would return to the shop. She always found it soothing to the nerves to watch the water tumbling over the weir.

As she stood behind a pillar on the promenade above the roaring water, she heard a

205

man on the other side of the pillar call out, 'There you are, sis. Well, the deed's been done. You might have performed the murder yourself.'

'It isn't murder, Alisdair,' answered a clear, high, arrogant voice. 'Probably only make them sick. Where was the delivery going to?'

Miss Hissop stiffened.

'The Countess of Carrisdowne, no less.'

'Zooks! Would you poison the very man I am trying to marry?'

'Relax, my sweet. Carrisdowne was reported to be in London when we left Brighton. It is well-known he never comes to Bath. You do not care madly for his family.'

'No, I do not,' said the female voice. 'The countess said in my hearing I was too bold a minx.'

'When was that?'

'Early this year.'

'Oh, the vengeance of Lady Clara.'

Miss Hissop trembled. This, then, must be Lady Clara Sinclair, and the man called Alisdair must be her brother. What had they done?

As if in answer to her unspoken question, Lady Clara asked, 'And how did you do your dark deed?'

'Well, as you know, we took turns watching the shop and found out the names of everyone

206

in it, apart from La Bascombe. So when you told me their servant was setting out with a delivery, I rushed back to our lodgings and changed into that Gypsy-woman costume—you know, the one I wore to the Pantheon two years ago. I followed this Esau and told him to let me shake a little lucky sugar on what turned out to be a centrepiece. Of course he let me, being as superstitious as any other peasant. So not only will La Bascombe be ruined, but very probably hanged for murder as well. Nothing like a touch of arsenic to brighten up the dinner party.'

With wide frightened eyes Miss Hissop looked down at the watch on her bosom. Five-fifteen and Henrietta had said the dinner was at five!

Miss Hissop slid out from behind the pillar and started to run. There was no time to go to the shop first. She, Ismene Hissop, must save Henrietta from the gallows!

CHAPTER THIRTEEN

The Earl of Carrisdowne looked quite satanic, as one elderly guest at his mother's dinner table remarked to her companion. He had arrived just before the dinner was about to begin and had been 'press-ganged' as he put it to himself, by his mother to attend.

His original plan had been to change out of his travelling clothes and immediately walk down to the centre of the town and seek out Henrietta. But the rain had begun to descend in torrents almost immediately after his arrival, and he did not want to be pestered by maternal exclamations over his desire to plunge back out into the storm. Because Bath was so hilly, very few used carriages and sedan chairs with the chairmen in dark-blue coats and cocked hats were a feature of the town. All the countess's servants were on duty at the dinner party, and to send a footman down into the town to find a sedan would occasion even more surprise.

He attended the dinner party with great reluctance. Sarah, he noticed sourly, was fatter than ever. The rest of the guests, to his jaundiced eye, appeared to be in their dotage.

Great cracks of thunder following blinding flashes of lightning made the elderly guests twitter with alarm. At least, thought the earl, the dinner would not last very long. His mother did not believe in multiple courses. The meal had begun promptly at five. Surely it would soon be over and leave him free to look for Bascombe's.

'I have a surprise for you,' he realized his mother was saying. She clapped her hands. The double doors to the dining room were thrown open, and two footmen carried in a centrepiece and placed it reverently in the middle of the long table. There were admiring oohs and aahs as the company creaked from their seats to gather around it for a better look.

'Isn't Bascombe's marvellous?' said the elderly lady next to the earl.

'I used to visit their shop when they were in London,' he said. 'Miss Henrietta Bascombe was famous there for her centrepieces.'

'It seems such a shame to destroy it, but it *is* for eating,' said the countess. She signalled to the butler that the centrepiece was to be removed to a side table and cut up.

Two footmen walked forward to pick up the confectionery; the elderly guests resumed their seats; Lady Sarah eyed the centrepiece greedily. Then before the centrepiece could be removed there came a sound of crashing doors and a female voice screaming.

Everyone froze.

The earl rose half out of his seat.

There came the sounds of a scuffle from the hall outside.

Then the double doors burst open, and Miss Hissop stood on the threshold with a footman hanging tightly onto either arm. Her clothes were drenched and sticking to her body. Her face was a bluish colour.

'Don't eat it,' she wailed. 'It is poisoned.'

'What is poisoned?' said the countess testily. 'Who is this madwoman? Take her away. Ladies, gentlemen, we will continue with our meal as if nothing had happened.'

Before the earl could intercede, Miss Hissop screamed '*No!*' With the strength of the mad woman the countess believed her to be, she shook off the restraining arms of the footmen. She hurtled across the room and leaped into the air. With a cry of triumph, she landed belly-down right in the middle of the centrepiece. *Smash!* Pieces of confectionery flew about. A cloud of sugar dust rose in the air and hung like a nimbus around the candles.

Ladies fainted and screamed. Servants tried

to drag Miss Hissop off the wreck of the centrepiece, but she clung on grimly, kicking out behind her at her tormentors with a serviceable pair of half boots.

'Leave her!' The Earl of Carrisdowne walked down the table and leaning down, peered into Miss Hissop's contorted face.

'Miss Hissop,' he said mildly. 'Are you trying to tell us that centrepiece is poisoned?'

'Yes,' gasped Miss Hissop. 'Lady Clara and her brother tricked Esau, our servant...shook poison over it...Alisdair is her brother, is he not?'

'No one shall eat any of it,' said the earl firmly.

'Oh, thank goodness,' sobbed Miss Hissop. 'They would have poisoned your family and guests and seen Henrietta hang.'

It all seemed to farfetched, so incredible. The guests were clamouring for explanations.

Lord Carrisdowne helped Miss Hissop from the table. She was a sorry mess, soaking clothes covered in sugar. He told the footmen to remove the centrepiece, to sweep up every bit of sugar, put it in a bag, and keep it in the kitchens.

'Will *no one* tell me what is going on?'cried the countess. 'Who is this woman?'

'She is one of the ladies from Bascombe's,'

said the earl. 'Go on with your dinner party, Mama. Let me take Miss Hissop into the study until I get to the bottom of this.'

They watched in silence as the earl led the now-weeping Miss Hissop from the room. Then as the doors closed behind them, a babble of noise broke out. The elderly guests were fast recovering and beginning to enjoy the unexpected excitement.

In the study, the earl placed Miss Hissop in a chair in front of the fire and then stood looking down at her. 'I shall make sure you have a change of clothes and something to help you recover from your shock. But it appears to me you have made a very serious charge. Begin at the beginning. Take a deep breath and talk slowly and clearly.'

Miss Hissop did as she was bade. Although she still strongly disapproved of the earl, it was wonderful to feel that the terrible responsibility of dealing with the nightmare situation had been taken from her shoulders.

She took a deep breath and began. 'I was walking by the river when...'

'Where is Miss Hissop?' said Henrietta. She opened the kitchen door and let in a breath of sweet rain-washed air.

'She probably took shelter during the storm,'

said Charlotte. 'It is only just over. She will be here presently.'

Henrietta leaned against the doorjamb and looked out into the weedy garden at the back of the shop. 'I do hope the countess liked the centrepiece,' she said.

'Bound to,' came Esau's voice from behind her. 'I was worried about it being Friday the thirteenth and all. But after that Gypsy woman sprinkled it with her lucky sugar, I reckoned that nothing bad would happen.'

Henrietta turned slowly round.

'You did not tell me about any Gypsy woman, Esau.'

'It was when I was on me road to the countess's. Oh, it was that hot pushing the barrow up them hills. She run up after me, and she even knew my name.'

Henrietta felt a stab of fear. 'And...?' she prompted.

Esau told the story about the lucky sugar and how it must have been very lucky because the countess herself had descended to the kitchens to have a look at the centrepiece and had given him a florin.

'There is no such thing as lucky sugar,' said Henrietta. 'Esau, if someone who wished us ill put something into one of our confections and one of our customers were harmed because of

213

it, then Bascombe's would go out of business.'

Esau flushed. Friday, unlucky Friday, would soon be over. Nothing terrible had happened. He felt he had been very silly in believing the Gypsy woman.

'I don't think she meant no harm, mistress,' said Esau.

'No,' said Henrietta, 'I don't suppose she did. The only person who has ever really threatened us is Lady Clara, and it's a mercy she is not in Bath.'

Josephine was stirring something in a pot over the fire. She brushed back a damp lock of chestnut hair from her forehead and said. 'But she is! I meant to tell you, but we were so very busy today, and...and...I saw a young man walking along Milsom Street, and he looked so very like Mr Clifford that I began to feel miserable again and could think of nothing else *but* him.'

Henrietta licked her dry lips. 'When did you see her?'

'This morning, walking past the shop. I am not exactly sure it *was* she, for as you know I never met her, but one of the customers exclaimed, "Surely that is Lady Clara Sinclair." '

'Do you think,' said Henrietta, 'that Lady Clara might have dressed as a Gypsy woman and put something in the centrepiece to dis- credit me? Something to make the countess ill?'

'No,' said Charlotte. 'I am sure she tried to burn down Bascombe's because she was jealous of you. It was well-known she had hopes of marrying Carrisdowne. But...well, dear Henri- etta, no one could possibly believe Carrisdowne has the slightest interest in you *now.*'

'I suppose not,' said Henrietta.

But worry nagged at her mind. And where was Miss Hissop? Henrietta decided to walk up to the Royal Crescent and just look at the house and perhaps watch the guests leave. If they appeared normal, happy, and animated, then she would know nothing bad had happen- ed. And she could look for Miss Hissop on the way.

Not wanting to frighten the others with her worries, she murmured something about go- ing out to get a breath of air. She took off her apron and, still wearing her shop outfit of striped cotton gown and frilly cap, she set out through the rain-washed streets.

People were beginning to move about again. As she turned into the circus, she heard herself being hailed from a sedan. The aged face of one of her regular customers, Mrs Cunningham, peered out. 'Miss Bascombe,' she called. 'How is Miss Hissop?' Miss Hissop was a great favourite with the elderly ladies who visited the shop.

'I hope she is well,' said Henrietta. 'She has not yet returned, and I admit I am becoming anxious.'

'I think the poor lady has had some sort of brain seizure,' said Mrs Cunningham. 'Just when the storm broke, as Mrs Brockett and I were sheltering under the colonnade, Miss Hissop ran past. She looked quite deranged, and she was muttering 'Arsenic...poison...' as she ran.

'Thank you,' gasped Henrietta. She set off at a run, the streamers of her cap flying. The Gypsy woman! Miss Hissop must have found something out.

Panic lent her wings. She did not stop to look at the countess's house as she had planned but hammered with her fists at the front door.

The butler opened the door, and Henrietta flew past him into the hall, shouting, 'The centrepiece. What happened? Have they eaten it?'

'No,' said a cool voice from the shadows of the hall. 'No, Henrietta. Come here. It is I. Carrisdowne.'

She flew toward him, questions tumbling one after the other from her lips.

Quietly he said, 'Miss Hissop saved us all from poisoning. Come into the study, and I shall tell you all. Miss Hissop is abovestairs resting. She has had a bad fright.'

They stood in the study, facing each other in front of the fire, each thinking how very different this was from the meeting of which they had both dreamed.

The earl looked very grand and formal. Henrietta, amid all her worries, wished in a very feminine way she was wearing something other than her shop clothes.

In a cool, steady voice the earl told Henrietta of Lady Clara's crime. Henrietta sat down suddenly, her legs shaking.

'It is as well I recognized her,' said the earl. 'For she did look deranged. Had I not been there, then I am sure my mother would have succeeded in getting the servants to throw her out.

'Although she succeeded in smashing the centrepiece, little parts of it had gone flying about the table, and someone like my greedy sister Sarah might have picked a piece up.

'The authorities have gone to arrest Lady Clara. The centrepiece has been taken to the apothecary's. I am sure traces of arsenic will be found. She is mad, quite mad. I began to suspect as much when I saw her in Brighton. And yet, earlier this year, I was happy to enjoy her company.'

'She was the one who arranged for Bascombe's to be burned down,' said Henrietta. 'I would have told you, but I only learned that evening...that evening you...' Her voice trailed away, and she looked miserably at the fire.

'Ah, yes, that evening,' he said. His voice sounded stiff and cold. 'I met your servant, Esau. It was he who told me you had already sold yourself to Brummell and Gillingham.'

'Esau? Nonsense. Esau is devoted to me. What reason would he have to tell such monstrous lies? And what reason had you, my lord, to believe such stories even if he did tell you such things? Perhaps because that monstrous pride of yours was all too ready to believe the worst of a woman who stooped to run her own shop!'

'Listen,' he said desperately. 'I admit—'

The door opened, and the countess walked in. 'There you are!' she cried. 'Ah, Miss Bascombe, you have no doubt come to collect Miss Hissop. Rupert, the watch, the constables, and the magistrate are all in the hall to see you. Lady Clara and her brother have somehow managed to escape out the back door of their lodgings, and no one can find them.'

'Very well, Mama,' said the earl. 'Miss Bascombe...'

'I shall attend to Miss Bascombe. Please

hurry, Rupert, and see to those gentlemen.'

The earl left. His mother signalled to Henrietta to follow her upstairs.

'I am sure you will find her quite recovered,' said the countess. 'What a drama! My dinner party will be the talk of Bath.'

Which, reflected Henrietta bleakly, was one way of looking at attempted mass murder.

Miss Hissop, attired in one of the countess's best gowns and pelisses, not to mention one of the countess's smart bonnets, chattered the whole way back to the shop about her adventures. She seemed more overwhelmed by the countess's condescension than by any of the drama of her heroic rescue. 'Put in the *best* bedroom, my dear, and attended by the countess's own lady's maid...not put in the kitchens, which one would have expected them to do, considering our class of person...or rather the class of person we have become by being in trade. And Carrisdowne! So opportune that he was there. No one else recognized me, for although some of the ladies were our customers, I was so wet, so wild, my own sainted mother would not have recognized me!'

'Yes, we are that class of person now,' said Henrietta bleakly. 'It was indeed condescending of Carrisdowne to entertain me in the study when I was dressed in my shop clothes.'

'Yes, wasn't it?' said Miss Hissop brightly. 'And the clothes the dear countess gave me. I would like to be buried in them with a little note, you know, pinned on my bosom giving the name of the donor. I might get a better place in heaven that way, don't you think?'

'I can't think,' said Henrietta crossly. 'My head aches. Oh, Miss Hissop, you are a heroine, and I have no right to snap at you. I am an ungrateful girl.'

'Not at all. No one can call Henrietta Bascombe ungrateful. Think how this affair will help our trade? Bascombe's will be crowded tomorrow.'

'I have no doubt,' said Henrietta wearily, thinking that they must prepare extra cakes and sweetmeats.

'And Carrisdowne,' said Miss Hissop, peering at Henrietta's face in the darkness. 'Had you not told me of his insolent behaviour to you, I would not have believed it. So courteous, so nice in his manners!'

'Miss Hissop, it appears for some reason Esau told him I was a slut.'

'Esau?'

'Yes, Esau.'

'Well, blood will out. That sort of low person always betrays their origins.'

'Not another word about Esau until I question that young man,' said Henrietta firmly.

But when they arrived at the shop, Henrietta had to wait patiently while Miss Hissop showed off her clothes and told the astounded Josephine, Charlotte, and Esau of their adventures. Esau was white to the lips at the thought of what might have happened if Miss Hissop had not overheard Lady Clara and her brother. He went even whiter as Miss Hissop began to babble on about the Earl of Carrisdowne.

They were all standing in the shop. 'Why do you not take Miss Hissop up to the parlour,' said Henrietta, 'and hear the rest of the story in comfort. Not you, Esau. You stay with me.'

'Got pots to wash,' said Esau, edging toward the kitchen door.

'Wait, Esau,' commanded Henrietta sharply. The others threw her curious looks as they made their way out.

Henrietta waited in silence until she was sure they were all settled upstairs in the parlour. Then she turned to Esau. 'Why?' she said. 'Why did you tell Carrisdowne those filthy lies.'

Esau fell to his knees, a miserable-looking figure.

'I am waiting,' said Henrietta sternly.

'I was frightened,' said Esau. 'I thought if

you married, then I would be sent back to the workhouse. I wasn't to get me wages until June. All I wanted to do was to put off the engagement until then. Oh, mistress, you don't know the fear o' the workhouse, the smell, the hunger, the cold. How was I to know you wouldn't cast me off? I never met anyone like you afore. In the workhouse, we're mean and savage like beasts cos that's what being poor does to a body. You got to care for no one but yourself. For if you don't, you die.'

He burst into tears, bending his head to the floor and covering his face with his hands.

'You did wrong,' said Henrietta. 'You must never tell lies again, Esau.'

Tears were pouring through Esau's fingers.

'Oh, don't cry, Esau,' sighed Henrietta. 'If only you had told me...But he believed you, and I do not want any man who would believe such things of me.' She walked over to him and drew him to his feet. 'Do not cry anymore. Go to your room, and pray that tomorrow will bring a new life, new hope, and a new Esau.'

When Esau had stumbled from the room, Henrietta took off her cap and tossed it on the counter. With her hands on her hips, she surveyed the shop. 'This is my domain,' she said aloud. 'I never really accepted it. But here I am, Henrietta Bascombe, spinster of Bath and shopkeeper for life.'

She went into the kitchen, took her sheaf of recipes, and sat down at the kitchen table and began to read through them.

She had not been so ambitious in Bath as she had been in London with the confections. But tomorrow would be a bumper day. She was a shopkeeper. She must cash in on her notoriety.

Josephine and Charlotte came in, asking if they could help, but Henrietta wanted to be alone and sent them to bed.

Josephine stopped outside the door of her room. 'She looks so grim,' she whispered to Charlotte. 'When I heard Carrisdowne was there, I could not help hoping...'

Charlotte miserably shook her head. 'There is no hope in Henrietta's face, and that means no hope for us.'

Henrietta worked on, glad to be alone, glad to have her work to keep her thoughts at bay. It was approaching midnight when she heard a gentle tap at the shop door.

Lady Clara! That was Henrietta's first terrified shock. Then she told herself that with the law looking for her, it would be unlikely that Lady Clara would call at Bascombe's. But Lady Clara *must* be mad, and who knew what a madwoman would do next?

Henrietta walked softly through the open kitchen door into the shop. She had turned the back shop into a kitchen rather than to have to work in the original kitchen, which was in an airless basement.

'Who is there?' she called softly.

'Carrisdowne.'

Henrietta opened the door.

'What do you want, my lord?' she demanded, barring the way. 'The others are asleep.'

'Oh, let me in,' he said wearily. 'I have much to tell you..'

'Very well.' Her voice was curt. 'Come into the kitchen. I can continue my work while you talk.'

He followed her into the kitchen. Lips primed into a firm line, Henrietta stooped over the fire, stirring hot sugar and fruit juice in a pot.

'Turn around,' he commanded. 'I must see your face.'

Henrietta carefully removed the spoon from the pot and laid it on the hob. She turned about, arms folded. 'Yes?' she said coldly.

'What I want to say to you is...what I must tell you. Damn it, Henrietta, my heart has been breaking, and you must say you will be my wife, because I love you; so don't stand there glaring at me, or I will *shake* you.'

'You believed all those lies Esau told you.'

'Pride. Wretched pride. What did I know of you? Henrietta, let me put it another way. If you do not forgive me and marry me, I shall wring your neck!'

Henrietta stood staring at him. He strode up to her and took her by the shoulders. 'Well, what is it?' he said harshly. 'A wrung neck, or marriage.'

'Oh, Rupert,' sighed Henrietta. 'Yes.'

'Thank you,' he said formally. 'Now, take note of my restraint, Henrietta. I am not about to kiss you and maul you. I respect you.'

'When will we be married?' asked Henrietta, her eyes like stars.

'Just as soon as I can arrange it. Send all this,' his arm encompassed all the pastries and jellies, 'to the workhouse. Bascombe's will not open tomorrow. You can take down that golden pineapple over the door and keep it as a souvenir.'

'What of Josephine and Charlotte?'

'I have already written this evening to Charles and Guy. I am sure they will arrive with all possible speed.'

'But Esau?'

'Surely you are not still concerned with that miserable, lying whelp!'

'Oh, Rupert, only hear why he did it.' Henrietta told him Esau's morbid fear of being sent back to the workhouse. 'And I still plan to let him run the business,' said Henrietta stubbornly.

'My sweeting, you may do as you please. I think one day I may be able to forgive Esau.'

Henrietta, suddenly shy, turned back to the fire and began to stir the pot again.

'Lady Clara has been found,' he said, and that brought Henrietta about to face him again. 'There was no sign of Lord Alisdair. Clara was found wandering in the fields outside Bath. It appears she has completely lost her senses.'

'But Lord Alisdair is still at large!'

'Lord Alisdair did what he did out of love of his sister. He is weak and shiftless.'

'Was she in love with you? Is that why she tried to ruin me?'

'I believe that to be the case. You would have been up on a charge of murder if it had not been for your intrepid Miss Hissop.'

'I have not yet had the full story. I know she smashed the centrepiece. Did she do it with her fists.'

'No,' said earl. 'She...sh-she...' He collapsed in gales of laughter.

'Rupert! What *did* she do?'

The earl pulled himself together with an effort. 'She took a flying leap and landed right in the centre of your confection and hung on to the table like grim death. Bath has never seen anything like it.'

Henrietta began to laugh.

'How wonderful to see you happy again,' he said softly. 'Come here until I kiss you.'

'You respect me,' said Henrietta, her eyes dancing. 'You will not kiss me or maul me or...oh, *Rupert.*'

He pulled her into his arms and kissed her breathless. Then he sat down at the kitchen table and took her on his knee and began to make love to her with single-minded thoroughness, taking them both off into the dizzy realms of passion while the golden pineapple outside the confectioner's creaked in the rising wind, and the syrup boiled over on the stove.